SHADOW FOUND

THE SHADOW ACCORDS

D.K. HOLMBERG

ASH PUBLISHING

CHAPTER 1

CARTH SWUNG THE LONGSWORD IN A SWEEPING ARC. IT was met by a thick-armed woman by the name of Jesse, who caught Carth's sword and deflected it downward. Carth didn't use all the skill she possessed, not wanting to overwhelm Jesse. Instead, she toyed with her. How else would the woman learn?

She had blunted the edge using the shadows, a trick she had discovered during one of her earliest training bouts, while wanting to find a way to actually use a sword as they trained. A blade blunted by the shadows could still hurt, and Jesse had many bruises where Carth's blade had struck.

All of the women of Reva she trained did.

Jesse grunted as she swung again, lunging forward, this time with an angry glint in her eyes.

Carth took a step back, sliding on the shadows as

she did, bringing her blade around in a swift movement. Using her sword this way, she was able to deflect the attack and turn Jesse's sword towards the ground. Swinging around, she caught her with the flat edge of her knife.

Jesse dropped her sword and raised her hands. "That's not fair!"

Carth sheathed her knife. She motioned to the sword lying on the grassy area where they had been practicing. The area was set in between two buildings, their high, sloped roofs arched away, making it difficult for anyone to climb across them. It would be difficult for anyone not in one of the buildings to observe what was taking place in here, and Carth controlled both of the buildings.

"That's just the point. Fighting is unfair. When you're fighting another person, the goal is victory. There's nothing ethical or moral about the way you fight. Someone stabs a knife into you, or cuts you with a sword, you'll die. Is your death worth fighting fairly?"

Jesse picked up her sword and stared at the blade, saying nothing. Dara made her way over and offered a wide smile. Jesse looked up and gave her a relieved smile.

Many of the women of Reva responded better to Dara than to Carth. Carth was too intense, though her intensity was well founded. She knew what needed to happen, knew that she needed that intensity. If she didn't have it, then others died. She wasn't about to sacrifice others for the sake of not hurting their feelings.

Dara reached for Carth's sword, and Carth arched a brow before handing it to her. Dara stepped back into a ready stance, smiling to Jesse as she did. "You just have to be ready for anything. Even if it's not what you think you'll expect."

Dara jumped, drawing on a trickle of her Lashasn ability, and exploded into the air.

A soft glow came to her skin, one Carth might be the only one to see. When Dara landed, she twisted, coming around with her sword in a sweeping arc.

It was a fighting style that Carth had taught her. There was a power to it, one that came from the way she utilized her abilities, drawing upon the flame, and augmenting her strength and skill. It was much the same as the way Carth used the shadows. Dara's skill had grown in the time since she'd been held captive. They didn't often speak of it, but Carth knew the captivity had triggered something for Dara, a desire to be ready so she couldn't be overwhelmed again.

Jesse laughed as she blocked Dara's attack. "That's… that's amazing!"

Dara smiled. "I don't think you'll be able to do anything quite like that, but you can be ready. You can learn to use your sword; you can learn to fight in such a way that, even if someone were to surprise you with an unexpected ability, you'd be able to counter it."

Jesse nodded, this time with less of the irritation she'd displayed when Carth had said something very similar.

"Now, let's try this again. I want you to be prepared for whatever might come your way. Know that you won't—you *can't*—expect all the attacks I might throw at you."

They began their practice again.

Jesse focused with renewed intensity, though Dara handled her easily. Dara had improved so much, but she had spent hours working with Carth in order to do so. If only she could reach all the women the same way she taught Dara, but she didn't have the same connection to them Dara managed so easily.

They'd been training them for the last month to build up skill, having chosen Reva as the next stop in their network along the coast. Carth was determined to have a thorough network in place as quickly as possible. It was the only way she would be ready to counter the threat of the Hjan.

Her claiming the C'than had been a start, but a dangerous one. Eventually, she would need to understand what that meant, though Carth suspected her claiming the C'than had been Ras's plan all along. The damned man might even have tricked her into believing she'd defeated him playing Tsatsun.

She needed information in these lands and Asador had shown her the key to obtaining it. Connections. That was the key for Carth.

The coast was the most logical starting point, considering ships moved in and out, and rumors spread quickly in places like this. Once she had her network in place, they could prepare to better know what the Hjan might intend. It was all part of being able to see the board more clearly.

Carth watched another pair practicing, their swords blunted by Dara's Lashasn connection. She could practically forge and reforge the swords using the power of the flame, heating it in such a way that the metal softened. It blunted them in much the same way as Carth did when she used her shadows on them.

Finally, she turned away and entered the nearest building. The inside was a wide room, as much apothecary as anything else. It reminded Carth of some of the herbalist shops she had seen in Nyaesh, filled with herbs and spices and leaves and oils, all mixed together and used in such a way as to help not only heal these women, but augment some of their abilities.

They were lessons taught to her by Hoga before she'd escaped. Thankfully, Carth had enough knowledge—and skill in mixing medicines—that what she'd learned from Hoga allowed her to empower these women. That was her intent. She wanted them to be stronger than they had been.

Had she not lost Hoga...

The woman was smart and had disappeared into the city. Finding her was something else Carth was determined to finish. The woman still had a penance to serve for the way she'd tormented others, sending women into slavery, essentially on behalf of the Hjan.

Hoga would not be pleased when Carth found her again.

The other side of the apothecary connected to a tavern, and she took a seat. There was noise and commotion, the kind she had known from her time in Nyaesh at the Wounded Lyre.

Carth listened to the sound of the tavern. It was a gentle cacophony of noise with familiar rhythm to it. There was a certain joy in being in the tavern that came from her experiences after she'd lost her mother and had thought she'd lost her father. They had been difficult times, but there had been safety in the Lyre as well. That was the last time Carth had known real safety.

Now she was in the tavern for different reasons. This was her place, a place where those who worked and served with her could help protect others. It was *her* way of providing a place of safety. Others deserved that as much as Carth had when she was younger.

She sat alone until the door opened and Dara entered and joined her, carrying two mugs and setting them on the table. Dara leaned back and took a long sip, but said nothing.

"Are you going to sit there drinking, or are you going to tell me what's bothering you?" Carth asked.

Dara looked up from her mug of ale, a hint of a smile on her face. "After what happened out there, I'm not sure you should be the one to speak."

Carth shook her head. "Me? You're the one who came in here sulking."

"Sulking?" She laughed and ran her hand through her pale hair. "That's not it. I'm tired. You have me training them hard."

"That bothers you?"

"Not that."

"What, then?"

Dara sighed. "It's been... too quiet."

Carth grinned. "I would think that after everything we've been through, having a little quiet might do us well."

Dara scanned the tavern. "I'm just concerned that—"

"You worry about that Hjan?"

Dara nodded. "I haven't wanted to say anything. I know how you get about them."

"And how do I get?"

Dara looked down at her mug. "You get... impulsive. They've hurt you. And you're scared of them. That's why you push." She looked up, meeting Carth's eyes. "I don't disagree with what you're doing. Far from

it. These women… they *want* the safety you provide.
It's just…"

"Just what?"

"That you need to see what you're doing. You
pushed me. Now you're pushing them. What happens if
you push too hard?"

"The only way to get stronger, and better, is to
push. Do you think the Hjan aren't doing the same?"

"There's the truce."

"Truce. They do the same thing as I'm doing.
They're planning their next move. They're moving
pieces around them. They're getting ready, the same
as us."

"They haven't done anything. There's been no
attack. There's been nothing."

It was almost enough to trouble Carth, but there
was peace.

And *she* had been the reason for the peace. The
accords had been her. Now she had to maintain it.
"Not yet."

"What if they don't?" Dara leaned forward, holding
Carth's eyes. "What if an attack never comes? When
will you decide they won't?"

Carth inhaled deeply and glanced around the
tavern. Her eyes took in women wandering from
table to table, a confidence to them they hadn't had
before. "Even if they never attack, our preparations
will have allowed these women—and others like them

—to protect themselves. If nothing else, that's valuable."

Dara nodded slowly, taking a sip of her ale. "It is."

Carth didn't want to argue with Dara about the Hjan. She didn't want to tell her that just because there was peace, the Hjan hadn't stopped preparing. Eventually, she suspected they would make another move, and she needed to be ready. Those she cared about needed to be ready.

"We've been here nearly a year," Dara started.

"We haven't been here for nearly a year. We've only been in Reva for the last month." Carth continued looking at the women in the tavern. The women of Reva had dark skin and quick smiles, making them naturals for what Carth intended. They were friendly, and there was an easy-going nature about them, one that allowed them to gather information.

It was like this in most of the places where Carth had established her network. She helped the women become independent, preventing them from being used, and asked only information—which they willingly provided—in return. It required an interconnectedness, but that gave them a sense of purpose, and didn't require them to rely on the kindness of travelers as they once would have.

If nothing else, Carth had seen during her travels throughout the north and the south that she couldn't simply sit back and watch as others were placed in danger. Too many places used women, putting them in a position of weakness. She would see them in a place of strength.

"Not Reva. But we've been in the south for nearly a year. Don't you think it's been long enough? When do you intend to return north?"

Carth cupped her hands around her mug. Returning north had always been the intent. It *was* her home, but that wasn't where she was needed. The A'ras protected the north. The Reshian, too, in their own way. Who watched over the southern lands protecting them from the Hjan?

So far, she'd seen no one.

The longer she was here in the south, the more she realized these people were in just as much danger. The A'ras had power of their own, even if they were somewhat limited in how they could use it to protect themselves from the Hjan. The Reshian, those who could use the shadows, were protected by the nature of their abilities. It was that ability that the Hjan feared, and why they had wanted them either under their control, or destroyed. Both were safe—for now—because of the accords.

The southern lands didn't have the same safety.

"We'll be here as long as it takes to get established. I think if we leave too soon, we run the risk of the Hjan regaining their strength."

Dara looked back down to her glass. Something troubled her, something that she didn't want to say.

"Out with it," Carth said. "Why are you focusing on our return?"

"It's… it's my sister. Not only my sister, but all of my family. We've been away for so long. At first it wasn't an issue. I thought we would return, so I didn't worry about it. But the longer we're here, the easier it is to remain."

Carth met her gaze. "I didn't realize being away bothered you."

"It didn't. Not at first. There is so much that I wanted to learn, that you could teach me. And I've grown so much in my skills. But…"

Carth nodded. She knew where this was going. It was different for her. She'd been alone since she was twelve. She had spent time on the streets, living in a place like the Wounded Lyre, and then moving on to train with the A'ras, but even that had not been home. Then, when she had left the city, presumably to train with the Reshian, she had been abducted, once more forced on her own.

Now she no longer felt as if there were a real place for her to call home. Home was wherever she happened to be, and for the most part, home was aboard the ship. It was the kind of home she could move from port to port, a place that was fitting for her. Even when she'd been younger, even when her parents had still lived, she had moved from place to place, traveling, never settling, all because the Hjan had chosen to destroy Ih-lash.

Carth should be resentful, and a part of her *was* resentful. She had wanted only to know peace and relaxation, but it was something she had never been allowed to have. She would never be able to settle down, to know the warmth of a hearth in a home. Yet at the same time, had she not wandered from Ih-lash, had she not lost her parents, had she not been forced to work with the A'ras and face the danger of the Hjan, would she ever have learned what she was capable of doing? Would she ever have helped as many people as she had?

Carth was not foolish enough to be thankful for what the Hjan had done, but she *was* aware enough to recognize that what had come from it was not all bad. In fact, the Hjan might have helped her become the person necessary to destroy them. And she *would* destroy them.

"I can get you back to the north. We can find your family."

Dara shook her head. "We don't have to change the plans you've made. I know what we're doing here is important. I just… I just want to be ready to return when we're able to do so."

Carth took another drink of ale, forcing a smile. "Of

course. When things settle down, I'll make certain that we get you back to the north."

The door to the tavern opened and a blast of cool air burst in with it. The weather had changed, leaving Reva cooler than when they had first come. It was a temperate place along the coast most of the time, one that rarely knew snow, but the rains had been cold enough for Carth to have needed to break out her heavy cloak.

Three men entered the tavern and took a position in a corner booth. Carth watched them with interest. They had a dark glint to their eyes. They were the kind of men she had known all too well during her activities of the last year, the kind of men who came to taverns searching for company, thinking they were entitled to it.

When one of the serving girls—a younger lady by the name of Hallie—made her way over to them, the nearest man grabbed the back of her thigh as she stood in front of them. Hallie casually swatted it away, only causing the man's smile to grow.

Dara started to stand, but Carth grabbed her arm. "They need to learn how to handle situations on their own. We won't always be here to protect them."

"But, Carth—"

"If we've trained them well, they won't need us. That's the whole point of us coming here, isn't it? *That's* how you'll get back home."

Dara nodded slowly and sank back into her chair.

The man tried grabbing at Hallie's leg once more, and she swatted it away again. She shot him a playful look, one that was both warning and threatening. It was a look that Dara of all people had taught them.

Hallie finished taking their order and made her way towards Carth and Dara. Carth looked up at her, a question in her eyes.

Hallie shook her head. "I think I might slip a little ferrace leaf into their drinks."

Carth fought back the urge to smile. They had been working with the women here, teaching them about the powers of the leaves and spices and berries, lessons that Carth knew a little about from her time training with her mother as an herbalist. The lessons Hoga had taught had been able to supplement these.

Hallie smiled again. "If nothing else, it will make them more compliant."

Carth met Dara's eyes as Hallie slipped back into the kitchen. "It seems as if they learned quite a bit. Maybe they're strong enough now to manage on their own."

"It can't stop. If we don't continue training, they could lose what they've learned. What you've done here is important work."

"What *we've* done here. This wasn't just me. The more places like this we visit, the easier it will be for us to keep ahead of whatever the Hjan intend."

Dara met her eyes. "I will stay here. I can help work with these women. They know me. They trust me—"

"Dara. You were just telling me that you wanted to return home."

"And I still do. But I also recognize how important this is. I recognize how important the work they do here is."

Carth rested her elbows on the table. She looked her friend in the eyes and saw the certainty in them. "We don't have to do this for long. Only until we feel confident it can be self-sustaining."

It was Dara's turn to force a smile. "You move on, stop in the next city you intend to establish, and from there we can continue to build your network. Like you said, this is important work. When it's done, we can return to the north together."

Carth shook her head. "The north isn't home to me, Dara. There is no home for me, other than the hold of the ship. The *Spald* has been the best home I've ever had, the closest thing I've had to a real home, since... well, since as long as I can remember."

"Then you take the *Spald* south. Continue establishing this network."

"Not south. Not yet. I need to return to Asador and check in with Lindy," Carth said.

"She'll be fine. You know she will."

"I know she will, but I need to check in with Lindy."

They'd been gone long enough and Carth wanted to

see her friend, but there was another reason. Word out of Asador was troubling. While the women in Reva might be safe, the same wasn't true in Asador. Carth had thought her absence wouldn't matter—not with Lindy in place—but it had.

As Hallie came back out from the kitchen, there was a certain confident swagger to the way she made her way towards the table. She set three steaming mugs of ale in front of them, dancing back away from their attempts to grab her. She didn't bother to swat at their hands this time, and the man with the sword no longer had the same anger in his eyes. They each took long sips from their mugs, and Carth counted to ten, watching as the leaves took effect and waves of relaxation washed through them.

These women would be safe here, and having Dara here would ensure that safety. It would also provide her with the point of contact—both of which were reasons for her to do this.

Carth dragged her gaze away from Hallie and nodded. "Keep in contact with Asador. It'll be easier for me to get word from there."

CHAPTER 2

CARTH WANDERED THE STREETS OF ASADOR, MUCH MORE comfortable now than she had been the first time she had come to the city. Troubled thoughts plagued her, leaving her feeling alone... and lonely.

The first time she'd been here, there had almost been a sense of desperation. They had docked, looking for help for Dara, who had been poisoned along the way by Guya. It had taken Carth's capture and subsequent freedom before she had been able to help her friend, and during that time, she had helped many others.

That had been the start of her forming a network of women, one where she was determined to see that no others were harmed the way Dara had been and to make sure that no others were captured and sold into slavery the way the women of Asador had been. The way Carth had almost been.

Now she wandered through Asador on her own, much like months ago. It was strange that she should find herself isolated like this once more. Would she always be alone like this?

Times like this made her reflective as she made her way to Lindy and the others in Asador. It wasn't that she disliked being alone, but she had thought she would begin making connections by now, forging a home for herself. After her parents had first disappeared, she had made friends on the street, but those friends had not stayed with her once she began developing her shadow abilities. Abandoning Kel and Etan and Vera and Hal had been for the best.

When she had gone to train with the A'ras, she had thought that her burgeoning friendship with Alison would create a connection, but when it appeared Carth had sided with the Reshian, Alison had abandoned her as well. Even Samis, the young man she had grown close to, even allowing herself to begin thinking something more might happen between them, had betrayed her.

Perhaps that was to be her fate. Perhaps she would help others find their place in the world, making sure they were safe, and then be forced to move on.

She passed a row of buildings, all different shops than she had seen in Asador before. Signs were painted in faded colors, the street in this part of town more run-down. On a night like tonight, with the way her mind had been, that was as she wanted it. It was better to be unnoticed, left alone, rather than drawing attention.

Carth found the door with the faded orange paint on it and knocked three times in a specific pattern before pushing open the door.

The other side of the door led into a narrow entrance. There were two women here, both of whom would notice her presence, though she couldn't see them. Neither said anything. That was as it was supposed to be. She made her way down the hallway, not needing the light of the two lanterns on either end that both glowed with the very faint light.

Carth drew upon the shadows, sinking into them as she made her way down the hallway, and that allowed her to see more clearly in the dark. Drawing on the shadows in the way she did, she was able to detect other pressures upon the shadows, and she mixed an edge of her Lashasn power, that which the A'ras called the flame. Between her two conjoined abilities, she noted the presence of the various people in the room she approached.

Carth stopped at another doorway. She hesitated only a moment before passing inside.

Unlike the other side of the doorway, this room was well lit. Nearly a dozen lanterns glowed with bright light, each placed to dispel the shadows. The air had an antiseptic quality to it, one that was a mixture of different spices that created a certain bite to the air. Two rows of cots filled the middle of the room, a total of ten in all. All were made up neatly except for one, and on that one rested an older woman with a bandage up her entire arm.

Evie approached. She was an older woman, heavy-set, and wore a white dress that was practically the color of the bandages and the sheets. She had flat gray eyes with heavy wrinkles in the corners, but there was a warmth to them as well.

"Ms. Rel. You've returned. How long has it been?"

Carth offered a smile. She found it interesting that these healers would choose to refer to her by the same title Invar had chosen. "Long enough. It was time for me to return to Asador." Evie nodded as if there were nothing more to say about that, watching Carth with an otherwise unreadable expression. "I wanted to see if there were any needs."

Evie shook her head. "You made certain we have everything we need."

Carth looked around. She hadn't made sure they had everything they needed, but she was trying to support them as much as possible. Lindy provided support to the healers while Carth was out of the city, and Carth had been more than happy to leave Lindy in charge of the city. Someone had been needed. Without support, this place of healing would fail.

It was unique in the city of Asador, likely unique other places as well. Carth hated that it was necessary, but places like this were necessary in every city she'd ever visited. Establishing a place of safety had been the first thing she knew needed to be done. She had to make certain that women who lived in the city, women who had been abused, had a place to turn, even if they didn't know it.

That was the first step in getting them to safety. It wouldn't be real safety unless they could recover. Carth knew that, which was why she had sought out women like Evie, women who had particular gifts with healing.

It had been Hoga—her penance for what she'd done and how she'd used women. Now Hoga had disappeared. She would see the woman back under her control before she did anything else that harmed others.

"Do you have everything you need?" Carth asked Evie.

Evie stopped in front of the woman lying on the cot. She unwrapped the dressing, and Carth noted extensive burns up and down her arm. It was a measure of either the woman's injury, or the sedation Evie used, that she didn't moan or cry out.

"We have almost everything we need. You made certain we have access to supply of herbs and powders, and we have plenty of funds. It's unfortunate there is still such a need for these services."

Carth nodded. She hadn't yet told Evie about the next step in her plans, one that would require even more of their intervention. If Carth had her way, they would continue to develop connections, and that ran the risk of additional injuries. If it resulted in information, Carth thought that would be worth it. She hoped those who worked with her thought the same.

"What happened to her?"

Evie finished wrapping the bandage along the woman's arms. "This one? She worked in a place where her master seemed to think he could punish her by shoving her arm into a vat of hot oil."

Anger surged into Carth. It was the sort of thing she had hoped to curtail. Would remaining in the shadows allow that to happen, even if women knew there were places of safety? Carth wasn't sure she was ready to reveal herself. When she did, she placed a target on her back—on the backs of all who worked with her. Was that what she wanted?

Safety. *That* was what she wanted for these women. For that, she would have to reveal herself.

But she still hadn't revealed to the C'than how she'd claimed them. Likely Ras already knew. It wouldn't surprise her if word had gotten to the Tsatsun master.

There had to come a time when she would announce herself, even if it was only to say that she offered protection. She had done the same with the Hjan. She had announced her protection of the Reshian and the A'ras. Was it not the same for Asador?

For that matter, she hadn't seen any Hjan in months. There had been rumors, but little more than that. She had discovered they were based out of a tower in a place called Thyr, and she had learned there was more to them than what she had known. The Hjan were an arm of assassins, but only part of a larger organization. The rest considered themselves scholars. Carth had little doubt about what they studied; they traded in knowledge of death and power.

"I'll do what I can to keep them safe in the city," she said to Evie.

Evie shook her head. "I know you will, Ms. Rel. All of us who work with you appreciate the fact that you use your abilities to protect us. Without you... most of us would be subjected to something much worse."

"But you worked as an herbalist before I found you."

Evie hugged herself, then ran her hands up and down her arms, the wrinkles in the corners of her eyes deepening. "Yes. I worked as an herbalist. But even then, there was a certain level of violence. Men would come, demanding treatments, expecting that I would provide them. Most would pay... but it was the ones who didn't who really worried me. Worse were the men who came seeking salves, thinking that they could force someone to do their bidding."

Carth started to smile, but she realized Evie was telling the truth. "What kind of salves are we talking about here?"

"The most innocuous were those who thought to make love potions." Evie smiled and shook her head. "It's not all that difficult to mix a cocktail that will put a man's heart at ease, no more difficult than making him think that it worked. Like I said, those are the easy ones. The ones who were a real challenge were those who thought they were owed something. They were the ones who thought they could use my knowledge in ways it was never meant to be used."

Evie's smiled never reached her eyes. "Those are the reasons I'm thankful for you, Ms. Rel. Without you, I would be forced to continue putting up with them. The local police had no interest in stopping them, and the alternatives…"

Carth knew of the alternatives. In Asador, there were guilds, but they were guilds of the thieves or assassins or even what claimed to be guilds of protection. Those were comprised of men—and they were always men—who collected their fee in exchange for safety. It would be one thing if they were simply hired muscle, but that really wasn't what they did, and few saw themselves as much more than money collectors.

Carth had dealt with several of them in the time since she'd come to Asador, and it had been necessary for her to take a more active role. Even though she had done that, she had maintained a certain anonymity. There were rumors in the city of someone like her, rumors that claimed she was attempting to consolidate power, that she intended to push out the thievers guild and the others as well.

Carth knew those to be dangerous rumors, but there was no way to avoid them. In some respects, having those rumors out there about her created another layer of protection. If people believed Carth was consolidating power, they might hesitate to move too quickly. By that time, she hoped to have a better-connected network. And then she *could* consolidate power, but only if it was necessary.

"Where is the other girl who's usually with you?" Evie asked.

"Dara stayed in Reva. She plans to make sure that what we've set up there holds. You should be pleased to note the women took to your lessons quickly." They were more Hoga's lessons, but she wouldn't tell Evie that. The healer had been helpful and had made certain Carth had the supplies she needed as she trained the women.

Evie nodded. "Doesn't take much to learn how to mix a few powders. The key is knowing the right combination, and the right time. Such knowledge can be dangerous."

Carth smiled, thinking of how Hallie had slipped the leaves into the men's ale to calm them. That was the kind of protection those women had never had. That was the kind of confidence they'd never possessed prior to Carth and Dara coming to the city.

"They're thankful for what you taught."

"Well, it's good to teach as much as we can. I just hope this lasts."

"What do you mean?"

Evie shrugged. "Only that when you're gone, we're likely to lose whatever protection we have, won't we?"

"Not if I have anything to say about it. Even without me, I want to make sure that everyone's established well enough they don't need me, that they can be safe without my presence, and without my abilities."

"How do you intend to do that? Not all of us have powers like you, Ms. Rel. And when you're gone, who's going to keep us safe from the Hjan?"

Carth didn't say it, fearing to admit it even to Evie, but she was hopeful that when she was gone, the Hjan would be as well. More than anything, *that* was her goal.

CHAPTER 3

CARTH REACHED THE ROOFTOP NEAR THE SHORE. SHE crouched there, overlooking the water, watching the waves as they crashed along the shore. Ships moved in and out of the docks, even at night. Some, especially the smaller ones with the sharp-pointed bows and the narrow waterline, she knew to belong to smugglers who worked along the coast.

There were plenty of smugglers here, enough that in her time in Asador, Carth had begun making connections with the various captains. She had been surprised to learn that Guya had not been as well regarded as she had initially thought. It troubled her that she had misread him so badly. Then again, how long had he been playing her? Possibly from the very beginning. That troubled her as well. Wasn't *she* the master of Tsatsun?

It was another lesson. Even when she thought herself in control, and even when she thought she knew what was taking place around her, she needed to question and make certain she knew *all* the possible moves, even the unexpected ones. Perhaps those most of all.

Other ships out in the sea had the wider bodies of longer voyagers. There were nearly as many of those, but most of them were anchored and didn't bother trying to sail at night, certainly not into the rocky coast of Asador.

The *Spald* was tied out in the deep water, and she had rowed to shore. She would need to find a crew, now that Dara remained in Reva. Lindy would help, but she suspected Lindy felt much the same way as Dara, and wanted to return to the north. At a certain point, she would have to start helping her friends return. That was what she had promised when they had first sailed for the south.

From above the street, Carth could feel a certain energy. It came from the city in something like waves. It pressed on her, moving through the shadows, filtering through her connection to the flame, a vibrancy and a life that only cities possessed. Villages she had visited had none of that. They were quiet, a place of calm, and oftentimes shut down shortly after dark. With Asador, much like it had been in Nyaesh, the city never really shut down. There was always activity, always something happening.

Carth listened in the distance, enjoying the muted cacophony of sounds, content to simply stand above the city like this. Here, this close to the shore, where she could see both the sea and the rest of the city, she felt connected to the life of this place.

She would need to get moving. She had promised Dara that she would continue working on her network, which meant finding another city, starting again. She would not have the same help she'd had the last time, but then again, Carth had always known she would need to do this alone. Her intent was to continue setting up an interconnected network that would allow her to know everything before anyone else. She would control the flow of information, and through that, she would finally know where the pieces moved on the board. This was the first step.

A cry caught her attention. It came from within the city, away from the shore.

There was a shrill quality to it, one that Carth had always been drawn to, the sound that she felt compelled to help. This time was no different.

Carth raced along the rooftops, jumping between buildings, augmented by the shadows. There were few who could travel this way, and Carth enjoyed the freedom of moving unencumbered by the crowds below. At this time of day, well after midnight, there weren't many crowds, but there were enough people that she was able to move more easily up here.

It wasn't just hiding from the crowds that compelled her to move along the rooftops; it was the fact that she could sink into the shadows and draw upon the A'ras flame, both without needing to worry about harming someone else down in the street. There was a risk with the flame that she could lose control of it.

She hadn't so far, but the more she used it, the more she felt it burning within her. It was a dangerous sort of fire, the kind that could destroy all of the city if she truly unleashed it.

The shadows didn't pose the same threat, but there were enough people who recognized the shadow magic, enough who understood the Reshian, that Carth preferred to remain hidden.

She jumped across a street and saw a woman lying sprawled across the cobbles. A young man crouched over her, reaching for her head.

Carth acted.

She jumped, landed, and, with her shadow enhancements giving her strength, rolled as she did. She kicked, sending her heel into the man's stomach, and he went flying backwards.

Carth grabbed the woman and raced forward. She heard a shout behind her and jumped, drawing upon her shadow magic most strongly, using that to give her strength.

She jumped, reaching the nearest rooftop, and ran across them. When the shouting stopped, she paused and set the woman down.

Carth examined her, searching for injuries. She found an angry bruise on her forehead, the gash still losing blood. She had dark black hair, and pale skin that reminded her of herself. She wore a dirty brown dress and well-worn shoes. A simple band of twine had been tied around her wrist, something she'd learned was a marker of betrothal in Asador.

She checked the woman's neck for a pulse and found it beating steadily. She breathed regularly, and there was no other sign of injury. She would need to be stitched, but more than that was likely unnecessary.

She could bring her to Evie, and then the woman could help make certain she was freed from whatever aggression she'd been exposed to.

When she was confident the woman was stable, she started along the rooftop, carrying her, but not moving with the same urgency as she had before.

When she neared the street where she would find Evie and the healers' hospital, she jumped, hurried into the building, and delivered her to Evie. The woman blinked, looking at her with disappointment in her eyes.

"Just because we had open beds didn't mean you had to bring me others."

"I don't think she's badly hurt."

Evie quickly ran her hands over the woman's body, finding the wound on her head before turning her quickly and scanning her backside. "No, I think there is just the one injury. That should be pretty easy to stitch up." She fixed Carth with a curious expression. "What happened to her?"

Carth sighed and shook her head. "I don't know. An attack near the docks. I had to grab her from the man who assaulted her."

"There are one or two of these each night."

Carth didn't realize there had been so quite so many assaults. "Are they getting to you for help?"

Evie nodded. "Your network brings them to me, and the others. We bind them up, get them back on the street. We tell them they have a safe place if they need us." Evie looked at her. "On the streets, that's what we're known as. Binders."

Carth frowned. "There wouldn't be quite so many attacks if they knew we were here, and if they knew that they had our protection."

"Or would there be more, thinking to unseat you?"

That was possible, and it troubled her. That was part of the reason she hadn't revealed herself yet, though not all of it. "I don't know."

Carth sighed again. That had been the intent. It

seemed that the more she saw, the more she experienced, the more it became clear that she had to make others aware they had her protection. Not just from her, but from those who were with her.

How could she remain hidden if others suffered?

She couldn't. That wasn't in her.

The only problem was, she didn't know how to go about spreading the word that she offered her protection.

She had an idea where to start, though.

As Carth turned back to the door, Evie hollered after her. "Where are you going?"

Carth paused long enough to look back. "It's time Asador at least learns that there are those who have my protection. If they harm us, we'll do as you said and bind them up. Then they'll be under my protection, and they'll be loyal to our cause."

Evie chuckled. "I don't think you need to prove anything quite so dramatic. Most who have learned about your protection have already become loyal to your cause. That's what doing the right thing tends to do for you, you know?"

"It's time for me to make sure that I spread the word."

Evie pulled the tray over and began stacking her supplies, threading a needle in setting it down next to some dressing. "Just make sure that when you do this, you don't give me too much more business."

It was Carth's turn to laugh. "I thought it didn't matter. You have a total of ten beds here?"

Evie looked up at her and met her eyes. "Ten for now. If things get active, I fear that won't be enough."

Carth left Evie and hurried down the street. She reached the corner and jumped up to the roofline, racing along it, drawing on the strength of the shadows to help her race more quickly than she could without it. There was almost a sense of flying, a sense of weightlessness as she moved along the rooflines. There was freedom here.

Carth found the street corner where she'd heard the girl's cry. There was still a stain of blood on the cobbles. Otherwise, the rest of the street was quiet. Carth pulled on the shadows, sinking down into them, cloaking herself entirely.

Up here, on the roof, such a thing would not look entirely unusual. There was a risk down in the street were she to cloak herself that she could make the shadows look too unnatural. She had learned to exercise caution when drawing on the shadows, not wanting to create strange contours to them.

When she really pulled, when she really drew upon her shadow-born ability, she could pull the shadows like a fog, darkening the entire street. It was something she'd only done a few times. It announced her presence, and those who were particularly skilled at detecting her type of magic—men like the Hjan—

would know that she was here. She preferred using her shadow magic in smaller increments, barely enough that others would recognize her presence, but enough that it augmented her abilities.

Carth dropped to the street, staying close to the building where she could hold on to her shadow cloaking and would not appear out of place. She studied the street, looking for signs of the man who had been crouched over the woman she'd rescued.

Carth had kicked him hard—hard enough that it should have knocked him out. Had he been with others, there was a chance they might've dragged him off and brought him to safety. Had he been alone... Carth hoped that he had been alone. She needed to find him to get answers.

She found him lying in the alley of a neighboring building. From the sign, it appeared to be a candlemaker's shop. The man leaned against the wall and took shallow breaths, his eyes halfway open.

Carth approached slowly, watching him carefully, but he barely moved.

When Carth had moved past him, getting behind him in the alley, she unsheathed her shadow knife. She stood far enough away that she couldn't be surprised by him, and crouched down so that she was at his level. Then she released her shadow cloaking.

It took a moment, but the man's gaze settled on her.

"Why did you attack her?" Carth asked.

The man coughed.

"Why did you attack that woman?"

He shook his head. He coughed again, and a little bit of blood-tinged phlegm came up.

Carth might've kicked him too hard. She might not get any answers from him. She started towards him but paused when she noted a loop of twine on his wrist.

It matched the woman's.

She swore under her breath. She had misinterpreted what she'd seen. This wasn't the man who'd attacked the woman. This was her betrothed.

Which meant someone else had attacked her.

Which meant… it meant that Carth had to find help for this man. It was her fault that he was injured—possibly seriously, given the force she'd driven through his stomach.

She sheathed her knife, scooped him up, and jumped to the roofs, heading towards the healers' hospital for the third time tonight. She intended to get answers, but first she needed to get this man help.

CHAPTER 4

"Are we going to talk about what happened?" Evie asked Carth.

Carth paced in the room outside the hospital, a hint of the antiseptic odor in the air still present despite the doors and walls that should have kept it out. How much of that odor lingered on Evie? How much of it was the hospital?

"What happened was that I made a mistake," Carth said. It really was as simple as that. Try as she might to come up with another answer, that was the only one that fit what had happened. She had seen the woman lying injured, unmoving, and had reacted. And now a man had been beaten while protecting his beloved.

"You can't make mistakes, Carth. You have to set an example."

Carth glanced over to Evie. It was good advice—

sound advice. As much as she might want to help others, she first had to gather information so that she didn't make poor choices like this again. It was all about understanding the game board, knowing what moves were happening around her.

"I know that I need to set the example. I'm doing the best that I can."

"And you are doing better than most. No one faults you for the anxiety you feel when you see others getting hurt. Gods! I feel much the same when you bring me each of the women that you have. No one deserves to be injured, not the way we've seen."

"You said he'll recover?"

Evie frowned as she nodded. "He will recover, but it will take time. You broke a few ribs. He'll be bruised. The other..."

Carth looked up. "What of her?"

"She was poisoned. The wounds didn't look life-threatening, but it will be difficult to help her until we manage to control the poison."

"You could ask Alex."

Her expression soured. "Alex is nearly as bad as her mistress was."

"Alex is nothing like Hoga. Alex has helped us." Alex had trained under Hoga, and had been useful now that they didn't know where to find Hoga, but Evie did not get along with her at all.

"Because you have forced her to help. Forced help isn't the same as someone who came to you willingly."

"Most of the women who are here were forced in one way or another," Carth said.

Evie crossed her arms over her chest. "I believe you know the truth of that better than most. These women —those who have chosen to work with you—are here for that very reason. They chose to do so. Do not lessen that choice. For many, it was the most difficult one they ever had to make."

She knew that she needed to be careful. Evie was right. Many of the women who now willingly worked with Carth did so because of what had happened to them. Many did so because of the way that Hoga had attempted to use them, and force them into servitude. Many did so because Carth had rescued them from certain slavery.

"I'll do what I can, Evie."

Evie watched her for a moment before nodding. She returned to the hospital, leaving Carth pacing, thoughts racing through her mind.

Carth lost track of time as she paced, trying to think through what she needed to do. Answers did not come to her, not as she would have liked. After a while —and she had lost track of just how long it was—Evie returned, a concerned expression on her face.

"What is it?" Carth asked.

"The woman. She isn't the first poisoned like this."

"She's not the first to be attacked, but the others haven't been poisoned."

"Jamie—that's the man you attacked—came around and said that there have been others."

"Has he said why?"

"He believes it has to do with the smuggling guild."

"Why the smugglers?"

"It seems the university has been squeezing them lately. The scholars there have grown impatient with the measures they are taking."

"I find it hard to believe that the university would employ someone to attack people in the street. Especially women."

"You haven't been in Asador for long. The university has often taken extreme measures. They prefer to control movement through the city."

Carth had experienced similar attempts at control in other places she'd been. It never went well. Anytime a ruling faction attempted to control another faction, some sort of underground movement became established. In this case, the university attempted to control the movement of supplies through the city. The smugglers charged less, and often provided higher quality.

"It still doesn't seem like the university would attempt to attack others the way we've now seen."

"Long before you came here," Evie began, "the university struggled for prominence. There is another place of study along the coast, a place in—"

"Thyr. Yes. I know of it."

"Yes, well, Asador has long had a sense of competition with Venass."

"Does the university in Asador employ assassins?" Evie arched a brow at her. "Because the Hjan are the assassins of Venass."

"No. They don't employ assassins."

"And I doubt they would be responsible for the attacks. There's something else to this," Carth said.

It troubled her, but almost as troubling was the fact that she felt like there was something she didn't fully grasp. It was there, but it seemed like a piece was missing from the board, one that was crucial for her to know the next move in the game.

All it meant was that she had to continue to search. There was nothing new in that for her. She often had to search for information. It was how she would ensure that the accords remained stable.

Carth would have to get Lindy working to find more information. Lindy had better connections here in Asador, especially after Carth had spent time roaming the coast.

"How many others have been poisoned?" Carth asked.

Evie frowned. "I don't know. Jamie didn't know. When his betrothed fell, he knew immediately what had happened to her, if not who had done it. Carth," Evie said, biting her lips and hesitating.

"They are doing this because of you and what you represent."

Carth suppressed a frustrated sigh. That had been her fear. As much as she wanted to do something to protect women of the city—as well as others—she didn't think that she would be able to do so. It would require more information than what she possessed. It might require that she remain in the city for much longer than she had planned. She needed to keep moving, especially if she intended to set up the network as she had in Reva.

"See what else you can find out," Carth began. "And make sure you get word to me."

"What do you intend to do?"

"All I can do right now is continue to search for understanding. I want to ensure that no others are hurt. That's what I can do."

It didn't feel like enough. And, she had regret about what had happened, about the way she had attacked Jamie. It was time that changed as well. "I need to see him."

"Are you sure you want to do that?"

She nodded. "I think I have to."

"Keep it short. If he gets angry, know that it's only because of what you did."

"If he gets angry, I can leave."

Evie arched a brow. "Can you? Are you willing to take yourself away from situations? That's never been your strong suit, though I can't claim to know you as well as some."

"What is my strong suit?"

"You've never hesitated to act," Evie said. "But there are times when even the most well-intentioned action has unintended consequences."

"I am familiar with thinking through consequences." That was the entire purpose of the game Tsatsun. Carth was a master at it, better and more skilled than anyone else she had ever played. She sought anyone who might have some ability, but had not found anyone who could present much of a challenge.

"You are familiar, but this is different."

Carth sighed. She would take time to gather enough information so that she could help the others in Asador. Once she did, then she would see that she paid back whoever this attacker was in such a way that he reaped the pain that he had sowed.

CHAPTER 5

CARTH STOOD ON THE DECK OF THE *GOTH SPALD*, staring over the railing, letting the shadows swirl in the darkness around her. There was a certain sense of relaxation from the shadows that came from her connection to them, from pulling upon the shadows, and she let them wash over her.

She didn't have the same connection to the flame. For some reason, it had always been different with the A'ras magic, though she didn't know why that should be. She had a connection to the flame, and could use that magic, and had been born to it much like the descendants of Lashasn were born to the flame.

She often wondered if it was as simple as that she had never known Lashasn. Maybe that gave her a different connection to her magic. Then again, she had not known Ih-lash, or even Ih, and somehow she still had a greater connection to the shadow magic. Did it come from the fact that she had learned the shadows first? Or was she simply more attuned to that aspect of herself?

Yet, there was no denying her affinity for the shadows. She always reached for them first.

Tonight they carried with them a different sense, one that came from uncertainty. It had been a while since Carth had doubted herself, a while since she'd doubted what she must do, but attacking Jamie had left her questioning.

Had she made a mistake?

Evie had made it clear that he would live, that the injuries weren't life-threatening, but he would require healing and time, things he would not have needed had Carth not brutally attacked him as she had.

She didn't regret acting. All the time she'd spent training, studying, preparing had made it clear she couldn't second-guess herself. Certainly not when it came to things like that. At the same time, she didn't like the fact that it was her fault the man was injured as he was. An innocent man.

Lindy joined her at the railing. "You're more silent than I'm accustomed to," Lindy said.

Carth stared into the darkness. She didn't know quite what to say. "I harmed that man. Because of me, he's lying in our hospital. I should've learned more before attacking."

"You reacted because you knew what's been happening in the city. You've been worried about those who work with you. Those are women you promised to protect." Lindy took her hand. "You did what you needed to do."

Carth sighed. She couldn't shake the thought that perhaps she had made a mistake. And here she was the one trying to set up a larger network. Perhaps she had not planned this as well as she'd thought. She'd believed that she played the game as well as anyone, but maybe she did not.

"Why don't we go below deck, and play a game?"

Carth blinked, turning her attention to Lindy. She was a beautiful woman; her hair—so much like Carth's own, and reminiscent of the people of Ih—was as much a sign that she was of Ih and had an ability with the shadows. Lindy had been a friend since Carth had rescued her. She had skill with the shadows, though not nearly as much as Carth, but that skill grew with time. That was not something Carth had expected. She didn't realize the shadow blessed could develop increasing prowess with shadows over time. She had thought it was something they were born with, and little more than that.

Then again, Carth's abilities had improved over time. The more she used them, the more she trained them, the more her abilities came out.

"I don't know that you really want to play Tsatsun with me."

"I almost beat you the last time," Lindy said.

Carth smiled. "I think you're stretching the word *almost.*"

Lindy shrugged. "If you don't want to play…"

Carth stared into the darkness. She needed to know what to do next, and maybe playing Tsatsun would help. The game had a soothing effect, one that helped her situate herself in such a way that gave her a chance to determine her next move. Perhaps Lindy was right, and playing would help her. Her friend always seemed to know what was needed. It was a blessing Lindy was with her, something Carth was very thankful for.

They made their way below deck and entered the captain's quarters. Once this had been Guya's room. It still held his bed, though the sheets and all his belongings had long since been burned. Carth had disposed of the ashes in the sea, something she'd thought Guya would appreciate. The man had betrayed her, betrayed those who had depended on him, and she wanted no memory of him.

The only thing that remained was his Tsatsun board. Carth had been surprised that he had one. She had since sourced a nicer one, but occasionally she still played with his.

Lindy made quick work of setting up the pieces and moving them into place. She had played as a child, having learned from her grandmother, a woman Carth suspected had been descended from Lashasn, though Lindy likely didn't know that. The childhood game had allowed Lindy to acquire not inconsiderable skill with the game, but Carth had trained with a true master.

Lindy made a move, sliding a Calvary forward.

Carth took a seat across from her. Moving Calvary first was a strong move, but it was not one that would lead to victory very easily. Carth had played that when she'd first attempted learning, and it wasn't that it was a beginner's move so much that it was a type of move that rarely allowed the necessary pieces to remain on the board.

Carth countered, moving one of the Shoevls into place. They were shaped like cats, though they would have been enormous cats were they to scale like the rest of the pieces, and she sat back, waiting for Lindy's next move.

"You don't need to be worried about what you did to that man, Carth. You're trying to protect those you care about. It was the promise you made to the women of the city."

Lindy moved again, sliding a piece they referred to as the Warden. It was vaguely man-shaped. She moved this next to her Calvary. The Warden could move in many directions, though not quite as freely as some pieces on the board.

Carth frowned, studying the move, thinking of

various possibilities. If there was nothing else that came from playing Tsatsun, it was the fact that she learned to anticipate, thinking dozens of steps into the future.

Playing helped hone her mind. It helped calm her.

Most of the time, she found herself playing against herself. There were few players of any real skill. There were times Carth wished that there were, but so far, she had not found one. Even Ras with all his skill likely would no longer present with her much of a challenge.

It was much like working with her shadow magic, or even the A'ras magic. The more she worked with someone with any skill, the more her own skill increased. Having the Hjan to face had helped improve her skill more than anything else.

Carth quickly determined the way the game would go. At this point, there were dozens of different ways the game could play out, but none would result in Lindy winning.

Carth didn't tell her that. Lindy needed to discover on her own which way her moves would take her. Having played as often as she had, Carth was able to anticipate the possibilities, calculating them in her mind.

There were times when she could do that in real life. When she had first managed to face the A'ras, the Reshian, and the Hjan, forcing the accords, she had done so because she had been able to think through all possible moves.

Now the game board was too fast. She was unable even to know which pieces were on the board, let alone figure out how they moved around it. That was part of the trouble. Carth could move them one way, but other moves happened around her. Before acting, she needed to know what pieces were out there, and that meant she had to position them in such a way that the game would play out as she intended.

It was a challenging game, and it was one she enjoyed.

Now that she'd figured out Lindy's tactic, she only had to focus on the game. Lindy continued talking to her, going on about plans and preparations within Asador. Lindy had taken it upon herself to make many of the plans for the city. Carth appreciated that she had, thankful that her friends had been so skilled at making these plans. It was something Carth didn't have the desire—or the interest—to do on a day-to-day basis. Her interest was in strategy. That was why she needed people like Lindy, and like Dara, to help. She didn't have enough people like that—yet.

Could she change that?

Carth started thinking that through. That was the question, wasn't it? She couldn't abandon Asador—she had barely felt comfortable abandoning Dara where she was for fear that others might harm those she cared about. Yet, many of the people she had trained had skill, especially Lindy and Dara, even if they didn't have the same level of skill. Carth had trained them, working with them as much as she could, but that had limitations. There was only so much she could teach, especially to those with limited magical power.

Carth made her final move, sliding the stone.

What if she could arrange for protection?

Her mind went towards Timothy, the hired assassin she had worked with when she had secured Asador.

There were others like him, she was sure of it. She had access to resources, and that would grant her the ability to find others like him, others whose loyalty she could buy.

There were risks to that move. Doing so placed her at the mercy of the sellswords. If they found a higher bidder, it was possible they would be swayed towards another side, but it was equally possible that Carth could first purchase their loyalty, and then earn it. If that was possible, then she wouldn't have to worry about her friends.

There was another advantage that came from hiring a man like Timothy—a man sublimely skilled with the sword. She wouldn't have to be dependent upon those with magical abilities. They could train Carth's women in more traditional skills.

Lindy set her hand on either side of the table and let

out a frustrated groan. "How long ago did you know that you had me beat?"

Carth met her eyes, noting the earnestness in her expression. Would she hurt Lindy by telling the truth? Would it damage her fledgling confidence? The woman had skill with the shadows and was more than an asset —she was her friend. She didn't want to damage that.

"Only a few moves ago."

Carth hated that she had to lie to her friend, hated that she had to be so calculating in everything that she did, but if she wasn't, she could already plan for how things turn out.

Lindy offered a satisfied grin. "See? I'm getting closer to beating you each time we play."

Carth forced a smile. If only she could find a true challenger. Then she could improve her skill, and then she would be able to find a way to develop herself.

Then again, if she found a true opponent, she feared they would try to manipulate her much as she was manipulating her friend, and the way she often wondered if Ras had manipulated her to the C'than.

CHAPTER 6

THE STREETS OF ASADOR WERE QUIET TONIGHT. CARTH liked to think it was because people feared she was out prowling—that they knew she wandered the streets—but that wasn't entirely likely. Her network might be growing, but it hadn't gained enough strength to be an intimidating force, certainly not in a city like Asador.

She had spent the last few hours checking on the couple in the hospital. The man was recovering, the wounds Carth had inflicted significant but not life-threatening. The wounds to the woman were more difficult. Carth didn't exactly know what had happened to her, and the healers couldn't tell either. Evie was a skilled healer, but there were limits to her abilities, and she claimed that whatever had happened to this woman needed a defter touch then she possessed. Still, she tried.

Had only Hoga remained, they might be able to know what had happened.

Carth positioned herself in the shadows, looking for evidence of the rumors Evie had mentioned about the attacks that had been taking place in the city. They were indiscriminate, the kind of attacks that were mostly a display of power. Carth recognized them, having seen something similar with the Thevers while in Nyaesh.

Making her way off the street, she found an alley that ran perpendicular, cutting between some of the buildings. The shops in this section of the city were less prosperous than some, though there was a certain live-liness to them, a sense of vibrancy to them that other places just did not possess. Doors were brightly painted, though in places their paint was fading. Some shops had signs hung out front, leaving them swinging in the wind. Others had clear glass windows revealing the wares inside. Carth passed anything from lamp makers to seamstresses to bakers, lingering the longest at the last. The taverns in Asador served decent food, but it was nothing like what she remembered from her time with Vera and Hal.

There were other shops here as well. Some, like the metalsmith, caught her attention because it reminded her of supplies she needed. She had several well-made knives, including the shadow knife and the A'ras knife that she kept with her at all times. But she had need of a sword; the longer length would be beneficial to her if she faced others like Timothy. She hadn't seen any other sellsword since he'd left her months ago, but now that she knew sellswords existed, she had little doubt that she would encounter them again.

As Carth continued along the alley, she heard a scuffling and paused.

She leaned back against the wall, trying to draw the shadows around her. Night was her time, the time when she could use the shadows, where she could conceal herself. But night was also the time when the underworld of the city was active, and it would be night when someone thought to challenge her.

As she remained in the shadows, cloaking herself, she used a combination of her Lashasn magic and a hint of the shadows, staying hidden. The combined effect helped her detect whether there was anyone near her. It was a trick she had only recently learned.

There was much she still struggled to learn about her abilities. She had gone to the remnants of Ih-lash with the hope of finding others who could help her learn the shadows, but there had been no one. She had studied with the masters of A'ras, learning how to control the power of the flame, but they reached a different power than she did, nothing more than a memory of it. Only Invar could reach the true flame, that of the Lashasn magic. Even those few she'd met who were the descendants of Lashasn weren't able to reach it as clearly as she was.

What Carth needed—what she wanted—was to find someone who could teach her. What she needed was a mentor, someone like Ras, who could help her learn the intricacies of her abilities. He had taught her about Tsatsun, but had not taught her anything about how to use the power of the flame. She suspected that he had great knowledge in that area, knowledge that she could utilize, if only he would teach it, but he no longer had that interest, if he ever did. Now he served the C'than.

With Carth having committed herself to them, she could go to him and see what he might be willing to teach, but that meant abandoning Asador. She wasn't ready for that yet.

As she stood hidden in the shadows, reaching out in all directions with her powers, she noted someone near her. There was a sense of pressure upon her, and she froze.

She had detected something like this before. It was the sense of someone with ability—the sense of someone who could use power. Carth couldn't tell *what* power, but recognized that they were aware of her presence.

She relaxed everything except for her hold on the shadows.

She held on to that as a cloak, using only the barest amount necessary so that she could maintain that connection. As she did, she focused on which direction she could feel the presence, straining toward where they might be along the street. She had known there were others with power in the city but had not encountered anyone else in some time. Certainly, she had not in the time since she'd been in Reva and left Dara.

Nothing changed.

She slid forward, holding on to the shadows, but pushing them out in front of her. When she was first learning of her shadow ability, she had struggled to move with the shadows, and it was not until she had learned—and understood—that she was shadow born that she knew what exactly that meant, and how she could move with them. At first, she had cloaked herself before moving and then recloaked herself. That was inefficient and had risked attracting notice. Now she could move while cloaked.

As Carth moved towards the presence she detected, the resistance she had felt receded. She couldn't tell if they were aware of her, or if they had simply moved.

She paused again, maintaining her connection to the shadows and adding a hint of the flame. The power surged within her, giving her awareness of heat and movement. It was almost a signature, almost as if she could see without seeing. Shades of color flashed before her before fading as she released her connection to the flame.

Carth continued forward, creeping slowly, more

curious than anything, before releasing both her powers. She tracked someone, but never managed to get any closer. There was a sense of them there, but when she neared where she expected them to be, they were gone once more.

Tracking led her to the shore. Carth stood between a pair of buildings leaning precipitously close to each other, more ramshackle than many others she'd come across. A few people moved along the street, but not many. From where she stood, she could see smugglers, their eyes more piercing than the average sailor's. There were a few men who appeared to be traditional sailors, making their way towards the taverns after coming off the boats. Some were merchants, pushing carts before them. Even at night, activity didn't stop. Perhaps especially at night, given the nature of some of these men's work.

None of the men she saw looked like the man—or person—she had been tracking. She felt nothing in the shadows that would make her think this was somebody blessed with shadow ability, nor any change in air temperature that would make her think this was somebody blessed with the power of the flame.

There were other magics—especially in these lands —but she wasn't as familiar with them. She felt no flickering, that rolling nausea that she knew from when the Hjan traveled. There was nothing.

And yet, she was aware that something was

changed. That presence had been there, pushing on her shadow ability. It had been there in the way that it had moved away as she had made herself known.

That troubled her. Not only had she detected power, but they had detected her.

If there were others in Asador with abilities, she needed to know, especially if they had anything to do with the attacks. She hadn't discovered what was happening, but she would. And then she would stop it. The city was hers to protect now.

CHAPTER 7

CARTH WANDERED THE STREETS, SEARCHING FOR evidence of the power she'd detected the night before. Much like last night, it was late, the moon a pale sliver overhead, its light barely extending between the buildings. A few lanterns were lit on street corners, though none on the streets Carth frequented. A fog drifted through the city, rolling in off the sea, leading her to move slowly, barely needing to draw upon the shadows. The fog itself was enough of a barrier.

Carth held her shadow knife in her hand, clutching it lightly, but keeping it extended from her. In fog like this, she worried she wouldn't have enough warning to react, and wanted to be able to attack were it necessary.

She still had not heard anything from the smuggling ring she was trying to discover. They were out there, the man who led it was out there, and she needed to find him so that no others with in her network were harmed. Since the last attack, no others had come. Carth doubted that had anything to do with the fact that she had hospitalized the man after thinking he was involved, but there was something more in place—she just hadn't discovered it. Whoever had attacked that couple was still out in the city. The man thinking to draw her out was still in the city. And there was this mysterious other, the one who had some ability, but one that she had not yet discovered.

Carth paused at one of the squares within the city, looking at the narrow wall that surrounded it. She was struck by a resemblance between this square and the one she'd been in when her parents had died. She thought back to the day often, thinking about the way her mother had passed, and how her father had disappeared, leaving Carth to think them both dead.

The pressure sense came again.

Carth froze, turning slowly. She released her connection to the shadows, easing it back enough that she was no longer obscured by them. She continued to reach out with the power of the flame, letting it flow from her.

As she did, she detected a familiar signature.

Carth hurried forward.

Lindy waited near one of the neighboring shops. She was dressed in a dark brown cloak that stood out in the fog. She wore a hat tilted on her head in the style of Asador and remained cloaked in shadows, using her ability. It didn't obscure her very long, or very well, especially since Carth could easily penetrate the shadows with her shadow-born gift.

"What are you doing out here?" Carth asked. The fog and the hints of cloaking she gave to her words masked them, preventing them from carrying.

Lindy shrugged. "I only wanted to see where you've been going. You disappeared the last few nights."

Carth shook her head. "After nearly killing Jamie, I thought it was reasonable that I disappear at night. I need to find out more about what's happening."

"Why do you think anything is happening?"

The pressure of upon her abilities was still there, though it was faint. Could she move quickly enough, and stealthily enough, that she could come across whatever was hiding itself like this?

"They're attacking because of me," Carth told Lindy.

Lindy moved closer, close enough that Carth could feel the heat coming off her body. She had a floral perfume on today, one that she'd taken to wearing with regularity. Carth suspected she didn't even know how easy it would be to detect that scent, or how it would be traceable. She had a decent ability to smell the fragrance on her friend, but there were others with much more enhanced abilities.

"It's no more your fault than it is the fault of these women. All they want to do is defend themselves.

You've done well by helping them find that measure of safety."

Carth scanned the street. If only the fog would lift, she wouldn't have to hold on to the presence of the flame quite as much. "Is it safety? Have I really given them safety, or have I turned them into a target of sorts?"

Lindy smiled. When she did, she was quite lovely. Carth understood why many of the tavern patrons were drawn to her. She had the soft, exquisite features of someone from Ih-lash. Carth's were a bit more severe, made even more severe over time as she had kept her hair short and hardened her body through training. She wasn't interested in attracting men, not the way she'd once had even a passing fancy in Samis.

"So much of what you're doing is beneficial," Lindy said. "You're giving these women hope. Many of them have suffered. Many have been used. Many have feared abduction and slavery, forced servitude in ways they could not have imagined. Before you came, they were unable to defend themselves, unable to protect themselves. You have given them that."

Carth wondered if that was true. Had she made their lives better by coming to Asador and setting up these women as her spy network? Had that really improve their lots in life?

"Besides," Lindy said, "you can't decide on their behalf. These women are acting of their own volition.

They choose what they do, not us. You've not forced any of them to act. You've given them a choice. It was more than they had before you came."

Carth sighed. Had she really given them a choice? Was it the same kind of choice she'd given Dara and Lindy, dragging them away from the north, forcing them into her network? Dara at least had chosen to remain with her, and now that she remained in Reva, she served in a way that Carth had never expected.

Even Lindy had begun taking on a different role. Her work in Asador had been critical in establishing the hospital, as well as establishing the network of women. Without Lindy, Carth didn't think she would be able to keep things organized. Her friend was a steadying presence, one far more than she let on.

"There is one thing," Lindy said.

"What is it?"

"We're setting these women up, and we're giving them knowledge and skill with these herbs and powder —enough knowledge that they can use it to counter some of the effects of the Hjan. But…"

"But what?"

"Sometimes powders and conversation aren't enough. Sometimes you need to act with force. Like you."

"We're trying to train them," Carth said.

Lindy shook her head. "There's only so much we can do. There's only so much I know. If you could work with them more, they might be able to learn what they need, but…"

"But we both know that I'm busy," Carth said.

Lindy nodded. "You're busy. I think that's another element of their education that we need to offer. You wouldn't have to force them to train, but you could demonstrate what they need to know. If they're able to defend themselves, they will be better equipped to provide us with the information we need."

"I'll offer it to them," Carth said.

Lindy smiled as if she hadn't expected anything else. And maybe she hadn't. She knew Carth well and had become very good friend to her. Carth trusted her enough to keep Asador running smoothly while she took care of other aspects of her plan.

"You should return to the tavern," Lindy said. "It's too foggy to see anything else tonight."

Carth took a deep breath, letting it out slowly. It was too foggy, but that didn't prevent her from detecting that steady presence upon her magic. It didn't prevent her from using the power of the flame to reach through the fog, to detect where that presence might come from. But Lindy watched her, a gleam of hope in her eye.

"I could use a game of Tsatsun," Carth said.

Lindy grinned. "Maybe this time, I'll win."

CHAPTER 8

CARTH HAD SLEPT WELL. SHE FELT REFRESHED, reinvigorated in ways that she had not in several days. Taking the rest of then night to play Tsatsun had done wonders for her. Lindy had needed it as well. It took her mind off the attacks they had experienced in the city, and off the work that still needed to be done throughout Asador, though both of them knew they needed to continue planning.

When she rolled over, Lindy was sitting on the plush couch at the opposite end of her room, staring at the Tsatsun board in front of her. She would make a move, then spin the table and make another. Carth had been working with her on trying to anticipate her moves, trying to plan for the next, and the one after that, thinking dozens of moves into the future. If she could, it would make her a more skilled player. But more than that, it would give her an advantage in anticipating what the various factions within the city might do.

Lindy glanced up as Carth awoke. "There was—" She cut herself off before finishing, a pained look on her face.

Carth threw the sheets off as she got out of bed, and looked at her friend. "There was what?"

Lindy sighed. "I didn't want to disturb you when Evie came. She told me to wake you, but it wouldn't have mattered, not at this point."

"What was it?" Carth asked. She suspected that she knew, the unsettled look in Lindy's eyes telling her that there likely had been another attack.

She only needed for Lindy to confirm it.

"It was Rebecca," Lindy said. "They found her near the docks, a knife through her eye."

Carth clenched her jaw. They'd found other women throughout the city injured before, though none had worked for her. That made the attack seem a little less focused. If Rebecca had been attacked—and if she had a knife in her eye—the attacks had escalated. And focused on Carth.

Did it have anything to do with the power she had detected in the city? There was someone else with abilities, but she had yet to find them.

"Why was she near the docks?" Carth asked.

Lindy shook her head. "I think she was trying to get to the smugglers."

Carth frowned. That wouldn't have been a useful way to gather information. Rebecca was a newer recruit and had come to them from the city, but she'd never been captured, not as some had. She had been spared that by Carth's actions. She had chosen to join them, and had a family she could have returned to.

But she was also inexperienced. Like most of the women Carth worked with, Rebecca was being taught observational skills, ways to pick up the conversations of others, to move quietly, in effect playing a game much like Carth had once played when she was younger. These were the scraps of information that she could use to build a larger meal. She needed those scraps to know what other steps she could take.

"What have we learned?" Carth asked.

Lindy set the game piece down; Carth noted that it was an Archer. The figure was well carved from a game board Carth had acquired during their travels, with the Archer holding the bow in such a way that the arrow appeared as if it might fly with the barest touch. Lindy twisted him, positioning him so that he faced inward, towards the stone.

"We haven't learned anything yet. We don't even recognize the crafting of the knife."

"Show me."

Lindy looked up from the board. "Carth, I don't think—"

Carth reached the door and pulled it open. "Is she in the hospital?"

Lindy nodded. "There's nothing you can do. She's gone, Carth."

"She might be gone, but I'm not going to let this happen to any others under my care. Too many have already been lost, too many who thought we could keep them safe. We've kept no one safe."

"Carth—"

Carth didn't give her a chance to finish, hurrying from the room, leaving Lindy to chase her out. She hurried down the hall, then down the narrow set of stairs, barely noticing the plush woven rug lying down along the hall, before reaching the other branching entrance and hurrying down that way, towards the hospital.

Inside, there was the now familiar antiseptic odor to the room. It could not cover the stench of death. She noted a hint of blood, mixed with another scent, that of the medicines and oils Evie used to try to repair those who had been injured.

Carth glanced briefly at the injured man lying on the cot, noting Jamie's bandages. He breathed deeply, and slowly. The medicines Evie had used on him were obviously effective. The bruising on his face had faded. Carth still felt a remorse at what she had done, but even that was fading now that she had heard about others being harmed. Wouldn't she take whatever action was necessary to protect those she cared about? Why should she feel bad about defending them?

She saw Evie in the corner, mixing a compound in one of her small mortars, mashing it with the pestle, working with a vigorous motion. Carth ignored her as she scanned the cots.

Towards the back of the room, she found the one she sought. There, lying motionless upon it, was Rebecca.

She was a mousy-looking girl, looking even more timid in her death. She had dirty brown hair, tangled even now. Her freckled face had a few scars, and dried blood streaked down her left cheek. An empty socket remained where her eye had been. The knife had pierced all the way through her eye, where it would've penetrated deeply, reaching all the way into her brain, likely killing her instantly. That was a small blessing. If nothing else, Rebecca had died quickly.

"Where's the knife?" she asked as Evie came over to her.

Evie wiped a towel across her hands, drying some liquid from them. Acidic, from the scent of it. Possibly an oil, though Evie often mixed some of the leaves into water, leeching away the oils within them, diluting them so that they would not be quite as caustic as they would otherwise.

"There's nothing you will learn from this, Carth. She's gone."

Carth looked up from Rebecca's lifeless body and met Evie's eyes. "Where is the knife?"

Evie met her gaze for a moment before shaking her head and turning her attention to the narrow shelves lining the wall. She hurried over and grabbed something with the toweled hand before returning and extending it out to Carth. When Carth reached for it, Eddie slapped her hand with her free one.

"Gloved hand or nothing," Evie said. "The damned blade is poisoned."

"Poisoned? A knife doesn't need to be poisoned when it pierces someone's eye." She kept her hand away from the blade of the knife, not wanting to touch it.

Evie carried it to the table and laid it next to Rebecca. "The poison is for the times the knife doesn't strike true. Even a single nick can become serious enough to kill."

"Do you know what poison they used?" The type of poison might give them some idea about who had attacked Rebecca. If they could find that, then maybe Carth could trace it back to the person. Maybe she could force them to stop attacking. If she couldn't... then Carth had other ways of convincing them.

"I'm still investigating the poison. All I can tell is that it's fast-acting." Evie motioned towards the bowl near the back of the room. "Whatever it is, it's particularly nasty."

"How do you know it's fast-acting?"

Evie motioned her to follow over towards the basin in the corner. There, Carth saw a mouse, stiff and dead. The mouse had a single puncture along its side, not enough for any real injury, just enough that it pierced the flesh, leaving a small bubble of blood.

"Just the slightest cut, and the mouse died within moments." Evie studied the mouse, almost as if she expected it to start moving again. After a moment, she shook her head and tossed the mouse into a basket near her feet. "As I said, particularly nasty. We need to figure out what we're dealing with before we attack."

Carth suppressed her frustration, but Evie was right. She couldn't rush in, not if there was a poison that was potent enough to kill with barely a nick to the flesh. If she did, and if whoever this assassin was found her and got a knife moving in her direction, she could be dead before she had a chance to react. There were plenty of poisons her ability allowed her to burn off, but there were likely some she could not.

"My mother taught me antidotes for particular poisons. What if we—"

Evie shook her head. "There are antidotes, but that involves knowing what you're dealing with. Some are nonspecific antidotes, where it doesn't really make a difference what it is that's used on you, but others require you to know exactly what you're poison with. This"—she nodded towards where the mouse now lay in the waste bin—"this works so quickly that you wouldn't have a chance to react. You might not even have a chance to place a leaf beneath your lips."

She turned her attention back to Carth and gave her a beseeching look. "Please, Carth, don't do anything where you would end up getting hurt. At least let me determine what this poison is; then we can find a way to counter it."

Carth nodded, hating that she couldn't act, hating that it felt like a betrayal to the dead woman, but knowing that Evie spoke wisely. She could patrol the city, she could keep herself cloaked in shadows and hold on to the power of the flame, but whoever was out there, whoever had used this poison, knew enough that they didn't even have to reveal themselves if they didn't want to. They could attack, sending a knife, dart, or even a crossbow bolt, before she even knew they were there.

She had thought herself able to protect these women, and they *had* gained knowledge and skill, but it wasn't enough.

"Keep at it, Evie."

Evie returned to the mortar and pestle, began grabbing a collection of jars from her shelf. "Oh, trust me, I intend to discover what they used on her. If there's any way for us to develop a resistance to it, we need to start now."

"Resistance?"

Evie nodded. "Some poisons are potent, but you can develop a resistance over time. I'm hopeful that this is one of them. If we can, then you could move without worrying that something might happen, that you might get attacked without knowing where they are."

It was the best option she had. She had to trust the people she'd chosen to work with, trust that they knew enough, and that they could help her find the answers. Wasn't that why she'd brought them together?

As she left the hospital, she paused one more time to look down on Rebecca's face. She cared about all the women who had joined her cause, all of them who had agreed to work with her, hoping that by doing so they could create a better life, but she wondered—what would she do if someone she cared deeply for were injured?

What would she do if someone she cared deeply for were killed?

Carth took a deep breath and started away from the hospital.

CHAPTER 9

THE NIGHT WAS CLEAR, NONE OF THE FOG FROM THE previous night evident in the city. There was a hint of coolness to the air, but only the barest chill. It was nothing like the cool of Nyaesh, nothing like the snows of Nhalin Fjords. There was nothing even like sailing across the sea, feeling the rocking of the *Goth Spald* beneath her as salty sprays crested over the bow, leaving her soaked. No, it might be chilly, but it wasn't cold.

She wrapped her cloak around her, the layers of fabric shielding her from the cool air. It was a finely woven cloak, one she had acquired in Asador. It helped her fit in here but did not offer quite the same comfort as the fabrics she had once worn in Nyaesh. Those had fit her in ways that this did not.

Periodically, Carth checked the knives sheathed at

her waist. It was a nervous habit, but she felt better knowing they were there, and that she could quickly unsheathe them. She checked her connection to the shadows and the flame nearly as often. If she were attacked, those would offer her more protection than the knives.

Carth continued to remain hidden in the shadows, but she found nothing.

With a frustrated sigh, she released her connection to the flame and the shadows, disappointed that she hadn't felt any pressure on her abilities as she had in the time leading up to Rebecca's murder. It was as if whoever had been out in the city with power had disappeared.

Carth didn't think that likely. Rebecca couldn't have been the prize, but so far, no others with her had been harmed. No other women had been attacked. Carth knew she should consider that a victory, but it was difficult to feel anything but anger that someone out there in the city had been so willing to harm these women, had been so willing to harm her friends.

Carth made her way along the street, remaining hidden in the shadows as she moved quickly to a familiar section of the town. Here, with the bright yellow door announcing the herbalist shop, Carth found the storefront she needed. She had questions for Alex, and it was time she had them answered.

Evie had raised the questions, making her wonder

whether there might be another way to move without fear through the city. Could she find a way to build up a tolerance to poisons, and if she could, could Alex help her discover what might've been used?

A soft bell tinkled over the door to the shop as Carth entered.

Alex looked up as she did. She was a younger woman, unremarkable other than her sharp nose. She had deep brown eyes, and chestnut hair that matched. Her dark complexion made her seem as if she had spent more time in the sun than she had in her shop, though Carth knew that Alex was nothing if not devoted to the shop. She stood at the counter, sorting through various leaves. When Carth entered, she grunted softly before placing the lids on top of the jars.

"Carth. Do you need additional powders?"

Alex had been the one to provide them with the necessary powders, leaves, and oils that Evie used in her healing. Evie was a skilled healer, but Alex had a different sort of knowledge. She knew how to compound the various components found in her shop, create mixtures that drew power out of naturally occurring plants, roots, even some oils. It was that knowledge that Carth sought now.

"I'm interested in a poison," Carth said.

Alex's eyes narrowed. "Poison? I didn't think someone like you had need of a poison."

"It's not for me." Carth shook her head. That might

not be quite right. "Well, it's not directly for me. There was an attack—"

"I heard about the attack," Alex said. "Evie came, looking to see if I might know anything about what was used."

Carth was pleased that Evie and Alex were willing to work together. Having the two women trust each other enough to question was beneficial. Evie's knowledge was more on the healing side, while Alex's knowledge had more to do with the ways the different compounds could be used. Both had their uses. And both women were incredibly skilled at what they did, though Evie had a certain distrust of Alex that stemmed from the fact that Alex's mentor had tried to poison and control too many women in the city.

It was part of the reason that Alex preferred to remain in the shop, separated from the rest of Carth's growing network. Carth understood, recognizing that she couldn't force Alex to work with the others, just like she couldn't force Evie to get along with Alex. They had to find some middle ground.

"Do you recognize the poison?" Carth asked.

Alex shook her head. "There are dozens of poisons that are fast-acting like that. But identifying them is a little more difficult."

"How would you normally identify them?" Carth asked.

Alex only shrugged. "Normally, I'm the one who's mixing them."

Carth started laughing. "Well, considering that's not the case this time, did you have any suggestions on how we could identify the poison?"

Alex came around the counter. She was a good bit shorter than Carth and quite a bit wider as well. She wore a long white apron, stained with a deep black, something that was almost like soot or ink, but Carth suspected it was something much different. Alex led Carth to a row of jars, and grabbed a couple. One held sickly-appearing bright green leaves that curled towards the ends. Another was a deep blue, twig-like item, and the last looked to be nothing more than sand.

"The felhorn leaves create a chemical that renders a man unable to move." She tapped the next. "This is terad. It's cheap, found all over the countryside here, and paralyzes as well."

Carth shook her head. "I don't think this was a paralytic agent. It was almost as if—"

"Watch."

Alex made her way back around the counter, setting the jars on top of it. She slipped on a brown glove and took something out from beneath the counter. Carth noted that it was the knife that had been used on Rebecca, but she'd last seen it with Evie. Alex reached under the counter again and took out a mouse, holding it up to her face and whispering something softly.

"Evie already demonstrated with a mouse," Carth said.

"She didn't demonstrate this." With a quick flourish, she punctured the mouse's hide with the knife. The mouse stiffened immediately and stopped moving.

Carth watched, horrified. Was that what would happen if a person were struck by this knife? Evie had suggested it would work that way, but seeing firsthand how quickly it worked was different than hearing about it.

"The terad works quickly. It courses through the system, taking the muscles' ability to move." She looked up, meeting Carth's eyes. "And of course, you need your muscles to make the lungs work, to draw breath into them."

"I thought you didn't know what had been used."

Alex opened the jar with colored leaves. She unrolled one, crushed it between her fingers, and stuffed it in the mouse's mouth. She ran her finger along its underside of its belly, stroking its throat. Carth watched, fascinated by what she was doing, and was shocked to see that the mouse suddenly took a breath.

"Narcass counters the terad. It's fairly quick-acting as well, but it requires that you know what you've been poisoned with, and that you have a chance to use it."

Carth watched as the mouse slowly began to recover. First it breathed, then its tail swished once, and then it began to claw at the air. Alex cupped the creature in her hand and placed it back underneath the counter, hidden from view in whatever cage she kept it in.

"When Evie described the effects, I suspected terad. There's no way of proving that's what it is, especially since narcass heals many things."

Carth nodded towards a jar. "So, we should send that with the binders?"

Alex shook her head. "You could send it, but it wouldn't do a whole lot of good. The narcass leaves need to be fresh to be most effective. They dry out fairly quickly."

"Then we'll just keep a supply of fresh leaves."

"That's the problem. It's difficult to acquire fresh narcass. We happen to be in the right season, and one of my suppliers found some not far from the city." She reached into the jar, unrolling one of the leaves. "This color is too bright for healthy leaves. In time, the color will become brighter and brighter until it begins to brown. Once it's brown, the leaves lose most of their effectiveness. It would be helpful, but I doubt it's the solution you're looking for."

Carth swore softly to herself. "Is there any way to test the terad and prove that's what they were using?"

Alex pointed to a series of liquids on the counter. "That's what I've been doing. Terad interacts in a specific way with roselin oil. I think this is terad, but it could also be ellswood breath. Both are equally deadly, but they work by different mechanisms. You don't want to make a mistake with those two."

Alex placed the tops on the jars, her gaze drifting to the knife lying on the counter. "I'll find the answer to this for you. I just need a little bit more time."

Carth nodded. What else could she do? It wasn't as if she could force Alex to work any more quickly. The woman knew how important this was, so she just had to give it more time.

"Is there anything I can do while were waiting?" Carth asked.

"What would you do?"

Carth stared at the knife before turning her attention to the jar of what she presumed was the terad. She tapped the jar. "Evie suggested that there might be a way to build up a tolerance. Is that possible with terad?" Carth asked.

"It's possible… but it's dangerous. I think you need to wait."

Carth thought about the image of Rebecca with her eye missing, the knife having penetrated it completely, blood streaming down her face. The idea that she might have died either because of poison, or because of the knife in her skull left Carth with the desire to do something. If it required her doing something that might be dangerous, she would do it.

"Show me how to try this safely. I would build up a tolerance."

Alex's face clouded. "If you do this, then you'll take all the narcass I have. I don't want you to die. The others need you."

"They need me now, but my goal is for them not to."

"Maybe. For now, you're essential. Don't forget that."

Carth only nodded as Alex began pulling the leaves from the jar and unrolling them before moving onto the terad. Carth watched, and listened, determined to build up a tolerance and determined to understand what she needed to do to stop the attacks.

CHAPTER 10

Waves crashed along the shore, and Carth stood atop the deck of the *Goth Spald*, feeling the rocking of the ship beneath the waves. There was a certain rhythm to it, a comfort that she had begun to appreciate in the year or so that she'd been traveling on the sea. It was strange to think that the ship was hers now, strange that she was now the captain, and in some ways, strange that Guya had been the one who had taught her to replace him.

Had he known that as he was betraying them? Or had he simply done it as a way to pass time, not thinking about the consequences? There was so much about the man that she didn't know, so much so that she wished she had answers to.

The ship was as safe a place as any for her to experiment with the terad, taking all but the barest slivers and mixing it in a solution of water to dilute it. That was the key, according to Alex.

She found that, with the first dose, she felt the effects immediately. Her throat seemed to swell and it took a moment to realize that it was not that her throat had swollen, but that her lungs had begun failing. Muscles in her arms and legs didn't work either. And the small amount of narcass leaf that Lindy had wadded up was quickly stuffed into her cheek, helping her recover.

The second attempt was much the same, though Carth had not strengthened the formula at all. She hadn't weakened it either. She was determined to continue dosing herself with the same amount of terad until it no longer affected her. The poison lasted for about an hour each time before it wore off completely.

By the third dose, Carth remained calm enough to realize that she still had access to her shadow abilities, and still had access to the flame. Using those, she was able to bolster herself, and quickly increased her dose.

Now she was several dozen attempts in. Each time the concentration increased, the effect of her throat swelling was immediate. She held on to the shadows, pulling on the flame, burning the poison from her. A part of her worried what would happen if she couldn't reach them. Would she be able to react in time, or would she effectively kill herself?

She didn't allow herself to dwell on it. Doing so would not bring her any answers.

"Do you think I could do something similar?" Lindy asked.

Carth shrugged. "You're shadow blessed. You're able to reach some of the same power, but I don't know."

"I think there's value in me attempting to gain resistance to this as well."

Carth hoped Lindy didn't have to experience this poison. The thought of her suffocating left Carth almost breathless. But if she were exposed, she *would* do better if she developed a resistance.

"Since I've proven I can withstand the poison for the most part, why don't we start giving you a chance to see if you can too?"

Lindy nodded grimly and took the offered terad.

They used the smallest dose, and Lindy gasped before she stopped breathing.

Swearing to herself, Carth tore off one of the narcass leaves and quickly shoved it into Lindy's mouth, forcing it down her friend's throat. As the narcass worked, her eyes relaxed, and she slowly began taking steady breaths.

"That's… that's horrifying," Lindy said.

Carth could only nod. What other answer was there but that it was horrifying?

"You're right. I think it's important we build up this resistance."

Lindy nodded. "It seems a blessing that Rebecca died from the knife rather than the poison."

Carth counted the remaining leaves, trying to calculate how many more times they could work with the terad before she ran out of the cure. With her ability to counter the poison using the power of her shadows and flame magic as it coursed through her, she wouldn't need to use the leaves herself. If Lindy could somehow master something similar, Carth thought that perhaps Lindy could use that to help her counter the effects of the terad. If so, they could use ever-increasing amounts of the poison so that they didn't need the narcass leaves and could preserve them.

The next few attempts for Lindy went increasingly better. She was able to draw upon the shadows, but still needed narcass to help her recover. Carth could tell Lindy was growing frustrated at the fact that she wasn't able to have the same natural resistance the Carth did.

"I think it's my combination of powers," Carth said. "I think it requires that I'm shadow born and have Lashasn blood." Maybe Dara would have better luck.

"We won't be able give everyone the same benefit," Lindy said. "Even if I develop a resistance, it won't matter. We could still be attacked, and those with us would be at just as much risk."

Carth sighed. That was her fear as well. As much as she wanted to keep those with her safe, she didn't think they'd be able to move through the city safely until they knew who was after them. She still suspected that it was one of the smuggling rings, although it could have been other thief masters in the city as well. There were nearly a dozen, all vying for control of their own sections of the city. They battled at times, some gaining more power while others lost. None seemed to fully consolidate it. Carth considered that almost better that they didn't. If that power were consolidated, they would be better equipped to challenge her and those she cared about.

Carth took an entire stick of terad, broke it off, and began chewing it. Lindy watched her, eyes wide, and as the effects began to work through her, Carth pressed through her powers, letting the magic scorch through her, burning through her blood, destroying the remnants of the terad.

She sat on the end of the bed, cupping her hands together, drawing strength from the shadows as she sank into them. She would gain power from them and did not have to suffer weakness of the poisoning, but what good would that do when she still had no idea whether the attacker was still in the city?

The city was quiet at this time of night, the sounds of the sea washing along in the background along with a steady murmur of voices, more imagined than real. A cool breeze gusted in, barely there, and carrying a chill and the scent of salt mixed with something darker.

Carth stood at an intersection of Asador, tense.

Something was off.

She didn't know what it was, only that she felt it and she knew it wasn't imagined.

She'd attempted using the shadows, and using the flame, but hadn't detected anything. There had been no sign of the strange pressure that she'd picked up either, nothing other than the sensation that something was off.

Carth tried to shake it away but couldn't.

Drifting along the streets, she remained hidden in the shadows, a part of them and separate at the same time.

As she went, she heard a soft scream.

Carth raced forward, drawing on shadows to give her strength.

The sound had been distant, and could be nothing more than imagined, but she believed it was there. The streets flew by and she hurried toward where she had noticed the sound. It *had* to be real.

Near a small square, she found a woman lying on the street. She had dark hair and freckles on her cheeks.

It was a woman Carth knew, one she had rescued before. Gabby.

She hesitated before heading over to her, looking around for signs of another, but there wasn't anything that caught her attention.

Carth raced toward Gabby, but could tell that she wasn't moving.

A small cut on her arm was the only injury. Carth didn't need to test the knife lying on the ground near her to know that it was poisoned, much like she didn't need to study Gabby to know what had happened. Carth had experienced the effects of the poison often enough to know what would have happened to her.

Helpless rage built within her. How would she protect these women? This attacker was skilled—and now had become deadly.

Scooping Gabby up, she carried her toward the hospital, knowing there was nothing that could be done. Tears streamed from her eyes as she pulled on the shadows, shrouding herself.

CHAPTER 11

CARTH STALKED OPENLY THROUGH THE CITY, HOLDING on to an edge of the shadows, and a hint of the flame. She didn't bother to hide herself, wanting to draw attention to the fact that she was here, wanting to draw attention to herself, thinking that if nothing else, she would draw this other out.

Now that there had been another attack—the first in several days—Carth felt renewed urgency to discover why, and to see if there was anything she could do.

She made a circuit of the places where her binders had traveled, stopping at each of the places where women had been harmed first, and then killed. There had been innocents, those who had no ties to Carth, and then they'd lost those who had come to her. First Rebecca, and now they'd lost Gabby. Both women had come to Carth wanting something different, though both had come for different reasons. Gabby had been one Carth had rescued from the caravan of slavers.

She had suffered enough. Why should she have to suffer again? Why should she have to die like this?

A slice across the arm. The cut wasn't very deep, and it hadn't bled very much, nothing like the brutal horror of what had happened to Rebecca, but the effect was just the same. Gabby had suffocated, the same poison coursing through her. Carth no longer doubted that it was terad, but even if it wasn't, she suspected that her ability with shadows and flame would allow her to burn off whatever poison was used, much like she had burned off the powders in the air when she'd fought Hoga. And now she was determined to find the assassin and discover what had happened.

There came a steady pressure, one that built slowly, growing increasingly strong the farther she went away from the docks, and Carth realized that she was heading in the right direction. Whoever was out there, whatever power was out there that could detect her, prowled nearby.

Carth didn't attempt to move quietly this time. What was the purpose? This person knew she was out there, and likely could detect what she was doing, and did nothing to hide themselves.

She hurried towards the sensation, letting it consume her. She reached out with the connection to the flame, focusing mostly on that, only drawing a hint of her shadow ability. Using it this way, she could trace a heat signature that seemed to pulse. There was no sense of flickering, nothing that made her think this was one of the Hjan. Which made it all the worse. At least with the Hjan, she had a truce of sorts, the accords that kept her—and those she claimed—safe. Whoever this was had no regard for the accords.

Carth gathered the shadows to her and then jumped. As she leaped, she used the power of the shadows to carry her up into the air, up to the rooftop, where she could stalk across the roofline, looking down at everything below her, using that to help her find who might be out there.

Carth hesitated at the corner, feeling the pressure of the strange power flowing around her. She didn't know why she detected it so strongly here but continued to stride forward, ignoring the fact that she was moving so openly. Rebecca and Gabby's attacker was out here. She didn't know where, but she knew they were here.

Following the sense of power brought her farther and farther from the docks. She jumped from rooftop to rooftop, scanning the street below her, searching for any sign that this person might be there.

In the distance, she detected a flutter of movement, one that seemed to come from all around. She froze.

What was it that she detected?

Carth moved slowly, making her way to the next

rooftop, and as she did, she picked up a sense of movement.

Far below her, she saw a strange twisting of the shadows.

Carth's breath caught. The only thing that would cause the shadows to twist like that was somebody who was shadow born. Maybe shadow blessed, but they'd have to be talented.

Was it Lindy?

Carth jumped from the roof.

As she did, there was the movement, pressure against her, and she raced forward. Whatever power it was that she detected was making its way towards the shadow blessed. Carth suspected Lindy was out there, but why would she have been hunting through the city herself? Lindy was skilled with using the shadows to conceal herself, and she had gained some skill with her knives, but she shouldn't be out here by herself.

The shadows retreated.

Carth almost hesitated. For the shadows to retreat like that, it meant that either Lindy had called them back, or...

Her mind raced through the possibilities of the worse things that could have happened. There were dozens of things that could have happened to Lindy.

Carth hurried forward, hopeful that none of it was true.

She caught a flicker of a cloak and unsheathed her

A'ras-forged knife. Carth called upon the shadows, drawing them around her, and lunged forward. She swept out with the knife, pressing the power of the flame through it, holding on to the darkness as she did.

She caught sight of something.

No, it was someone.

A man, with a long face and bright green eyes that stared back at her. He had short brown hair and a muscular build. He flicked something at her, and she twisted, though it grazed her shoulder.

Pain burned.

Poison.

Carth surged the shadows and the flame through her, using that connection to cleanse herself of the poison, burning it away.

She flipped her knife in his direction, sending it streaking towards him on the power of the flame. The man ducked, rolling away from her knife. She swore softly as it whistled past him, missing.

Carth rolled with him, throwing herself forward. If she had been uncertain at all that this was the man who'd attacked the others, that doubt had been answered by the poison on the knife.

She jumped, throwing herself up and into the air. When she landed, she spun, facing him from the opposite direction.

He twisted, dropping to the ground almost as soon as she attacked. He was a skilled fighter, anticipating her moves. His fighting style was nothing like any she'd ever seen before. It was all fluid movements, quick and powerful, enough that he could avoid her attacks.

As she kicked at him, and he rolled, she asked, "Why are you harming these women?"

The man jumped to the side just as she swung her knife at him. She barely missed him.

"Just a job."

"What was the job?" Carth asked.

The man flashed a wolfish grin. "Does it matter? It's been done."

Carth punched, swinging her arm around, and grazed him on the shoulder. It was only the barest contact, but it sent him spinning, spiraling away.

He dropped, her next punch sailing over his head.

"What was the job?" Carth repeated.

"A threat in the city I was hired to remove."

"Who?"

The man shrugged. As he did, he rolled out of reach. He was quick, fast enough that Carth could continue to attack him, but she would have to use the shadows in order do so. He seemed to know her fighting style, and could counter her movements and react more quickly than most fighters she had ever encountered.

"The job is done," the man said.

"Who? Who were you hired to kill?"

The man backed away from her, reaching one of the

neighboring buildings. He grabbed one of the over-hangs and flipped himself up, crouching there. He stared at Carth, his dark green eyes reflecting the night back at her. They reminded of Carth of another man with dark green eyes, the leader of the Hjan, a man she had learned to fear.

His name flashed through her mind: Danis.

Was he like Danis? Should she fear this man? He watched her, the expression on his face one of casual interest, not one of fear. This was not a man concerned about what Carth might do to him. He did not worry that she might harm him, and after fighting with him, she wasn't sure if he had any need to be worried about her. He was surprisingly skilled.

Carth gathered the shadows, preparing to attack him, when she heard a soft moaning behind her. She spun. As she did, a knife struck her in the back, sinking into her shoulder blade.

Had she not turned, the knife would have hit her in the chest, likely in her heart.

Carth staggered off to the side, reaching for the blade and dislodging it. She sent a combination of the shadows and the flame through the wound, pushing back the pain from the attack, burning off the poison that threatened to overwhelm her.

Carth glanced up, but the man had disappeared.

She held on to the knife, not fearing the poison on the blade as Evie had, worried only about the soft whimpering. She staggered down the street, pain throbbing through her shoulder and threatening to overwhelm her, sharper than any she'd experienced before. She reached a body lying sprawled on the ground, whimpering softly.

Carth's breath caught.

Lindy.

CHAPTER 12

CARTH STUMBLED TOWARDS LINDY. THE POISON THAT was running through her system was more potent than she'd experienced before. She had tested terad, but this didn't feel quite like terad. She searched through the shadows, sending through that connection to the flame as well, trying to draw upon their strength so that she could burn it off of her and not succumb to its effects.

She staggered to her knees next to Lindy.

The other woman stared up at the sky, eyes wide. Carth checked her neck, found she was barely breathing.

"Where is the narcass?" Carth asked.

Lindy couldn't answer.

Carth whispered Lindy's name. Even that was difficult. She could feel the effects of the poison fading, but it was happening slowly—too slowly. Lindy didn't move. Carth imagined her suffocating, much like Gabby had suffocated.

Carth searched Lindy, peeling back her cloak, looking for signs of injury. Her eyes scanned the street until she found a knife lying not far from the other woman. Blood stained the tip, and it pooled in a trail to her flank. Carth rolled Lindy, looking at the wound. It was deeper than Gabby's had been, cutting through the flesh, leaving a gaping wound. If poison, the wound would have given plenty of area for the poison to absorb. Carth slipped her hand through Lindy's cloak, looking in the pockets, then moved on to her pants. She searched for narcass leaves, but there were none.

Carth lowered her head to Lindy's chest, listening, afraid that her heart had stopped, or that she had ceased breathing altogether.

Her heart still beat, though it was slow. Breaths were taken, but they too were slower.

She debated where to go. She could bring Lindy back to the *Goth Spald*, where Carth knew there would be narcass leaves, but it would take longer. Alternatively, she could race to Alex's shop and pray that the woman had more leaves. Pray that there was some other way to help Lindy.

That was what Carth decided to do.

Scooping her up, she almost stumbled. Fatigue washed over her. The effort of fending off the poisoning was nearly too much for her. Carth held on to the shadows, drawing strength from them as she did. She managed to hold on to Lindy, keeping her in her arms.

Lindy moaned softly.

Carth's heart raced. She hurried forward, terrified that she wouldn't be strong enough, that she wouldn't be fast enough.

She jumped through the streets. Lindy was limp in her arms. Carth wanted to pause, to take a break to see if she still breathed, if her heart still beat, but she didn't dare.

Carth found the street where Alex's shop would be and hurried along it. With each step, she moved more slowly. Soon she was barely able to lift her legs.

Carth drew upon the shadows, but even that strength began to fade from her.

She wondered briefly why she should be so weak before wondering if perhaps she hadn't fully burned off the poisoning before expending her energy on carrying Lindy.

In the distance, she saw the faded yellow door marking Alex's store. She stumbled towards it, as quickly as she could with as weak as she was. She found it difficult to lift her legs, each step challenging.

It seemed a battle of will for her to reach the door. It was close, but tantalizingly far away as well. Her mouth began to grow dry. Her arms began to quiver, and she fought against the need to lay Lindy down. She wouldn't set her friend down until she was someplace where she could help her.

Slowly—too slowly—she reached the door.

Carth leaned against it. With one booted foot, she kicked at it.

It was late, and she worried that she might startle Alex too much, but what choice did she have? When nobody answered the door, Carth kicked again.

Finally, she heard footsteps on the other side. The door opened, and Carth stumbled inside. Alex looked up at her, her eyes wide, frightened expression upon her face.

Carth fell to the floor, finally releasing Lindy so that she rolled to the side, her head lolling over, striking the stone.

"What happened?" Alex asked.

"Attack. Don't know. Who. Poison."

"You knew there was poison on those blades. I warned you to give me a chance to find out what poison it was. I thought it was terad, but it's possible that it wasn't."

"Not. Terad."

"No, I can tell you now that it wasn't terad."

Carth's head sunk to the floor. "I. Expended too much. Can't. Burn it off."

Carth closed her eyes, unable to move. In some ways, it was like the terad, the effect of the poison racing through her, limiting her ability to function. In others, this was nothing like it. With terad, she was certain the effect would wear off fairly quickly. This had been going on for half an hour. Or longer. Long enough that she began to wonder whether it would wear off at all.

She felt her lungs begin to burn. She felt hands on her, but only vaguely. Reaching Alex's shop had been her goal. Now that she was here, she had no other goal. This was what she had wanted, what she had needed.

She heard distant voices.

"You should be dead."

That rung most clearly in her mind. Carth knew it was true. She should be dead. She had made a mistake thinking that she knew what she needed to do, but hadn't given the people that she worked with a chance to discover what exactly they were up against. Alex had warned her she wasn't certain, and Carth had pressed forward anyway. Because of that, she might die. Lindy might die.

Distantly, Carth was aware of something shoved into her mouth. A finger rammed deeper into her throat, shoving what Carth presumed to be narcass down into her throat.

"Last one," she heard.

"You know what she'll—"

"We need her."

Slowly, a wave of relaxation began to roll through her. She detected it as her chest loosening, as if the pain that was there had finally begun to ease. From there, her throat no longer seemed quite as swollen. Carth pulled on the shadows, drawing strength from them, adding to the narcass.

As the effect of the poison faded, she let herself relax, and her breathing became easier.

She opened her eyes. Alex crouched over her, worry written into the wrinkles on her face. Evie was there as well.

"Lindy." It was all Carth could do to say Lindy's name. But she needed to know what had happened to her friend, and whether they had been able to save her as well.

"We only had one narcass leaf remaining," Alex said.

Carth licked her lips. They seemed suddenly dry, almost painfully so. "One?" What did that mean, that they only had one leaf remaining?

Alex nodded. "I'm sorry, Carth."

Carth pulled on the shadows, sitting up. She was still in Alex's shop, unmoved from where she had ended up after stumbling in. The stone was cold, but Carth understood why they hadn't moved her. Doing so would have wasted time, something that was precious to them.

Lying next to her, unmoving, was Lindy. Carth didn't need to check her neck for a pulse or lay her head on her chest to listen for her breathing to know that she would find neither.

She scooted towards her friend, tears coming unbidden to her. "Lindy?"

The woman's arms were cold. Muscles were stiff, the rigor of death already claiming her.

"We only had one. I'm so sorry, Carth."

Carth didn't have the energy to tell them that they should have used it on Lindy. She didn't have the energy to let them know that she likely would've been fine, that she could have burned off the effects of the poison, and that using both of shadows and the flame, she would've survived.

How were they to know? How were they to know that she because of her, Lindy was now dead?

CHAPTER 13

THE COT IN THE HOSPITAL WAS CLEAN TODAY. THE medicinal stench was no different today, only today there was a scent of sickness in the air. Carth couldn't shake it from her nose, just as she couldn't shake the taste of narcass from her tongue, the bitterness of the leaf betraying her.

She stared at the cot holding Lindy. Carth chewed on a terad root, ignoring the effect of the poison as it attempted to work through her. She surged with her magic, drawing strength from it, burning off the effects of the poison. It was more concentrated than any other dose she had attempted. She practically sucked at the poison within the root, drawing it from it.

Evie watched her with her lips pursed and her brow furrowed. Carth ignored the glances that she shot her.

"Alex claims this was evenfire," Carth said.

Evie stood in the corner, mashing a compound together. She worked silently, her arms pressing with great force as she ground the necessary components. It was the concoction that Alex had instructed her how to make, one that might bring the woman some respite. The fact that Carth hadn't perished from the poison was surprising.

"That's what she says," Evie said.

"You don't believe that she's telling the truth?" Carth asked.

Evie shook her head. "I believe Alex. I just fear what you intend to do now that you know what the poison is. It's bad enough what you're doing with..." She watched the way Carth chewed on the narcass and shook her head. "It doesn't matter. You've been chewing on that root as if you intended to eat it for dinner. Any other person did the same, they'd be dead within moments. I think regardless of what I might have to say, you intend to prove me wrong."

Carth plucked the terad root from her mouth and tossed it in the bin at the end of the bed. "I intend to do what I can to find out why Lindy was killed."

"Probably the same as the rest. They were trying to do—"

"No. Lindy was different than the rest. This man was after something. He seemed to think that he'd gotten his target. And if his target was Lindy, I need to know why."

Evie set the bowl down and crossed her arms over her chest. "You go chasing after someone like that, you're just as likely to get killed. If Lindy couldn't protect herself, what makes you think the rest of these women can?" She fixed Carth with a hard look. "We need you, Carth. We need your expertise, and we need your strength. Without it… without it, I think we might be in danger again."

Carth sighed. Lindy had made a similar comment once, telling her that Carth needed to help them become stronger, that she could help ensure that they were safe, but it would require that she work with them. Only, Carth might be able to work with them, but they needed more than that. They needed fighting skill that she wasn't sure she could teach. Was it something she was *willing* to teach? Did she intend to turn them into soldiers?

She turned her attention back to Lindy, staring at her friend's unmoving body. She was gone. There was nothing Carth could do to bring her back, nothing she could do that would reverse the effects of the poison. The only thing she could do was get vengeance for what had happened to her.

Carth started to turn when Evie stepped forward, raising a hand. "What do you intend to do?"

Carth glanced to Lindy before turning her attention to Evie. "I intend to see that this man and whoever hired him are destroyed."

As she strode from the room, her gaze touched on the fallen woman. Carth needed to do this for all the women in the city who had been subjected to the violence here, but now it was even more personal.

Carth trailed the man from his ship. He cast a furtive glance around him, but she remained hidden in the shadows, concealed from him. She felt no pressure of him on her senses, nothing that would tell her that the assassin was near. She hadn't discovered what his ability was, but he did have some way of fighting well, and she wondered if maybe enhanced speed or agility was part of it. She had some of that with the shadows, but he had not been gifted by the shadows, of that she was certain.

As this man moved away from the docks and into the alley, pushing his heavily laden cart, she followed after him, keeping a close eye on him so that he didn't disappear from her. She was tempted to follow him from above, to use the rooftops to trail him, but she preferred not to catch him completely off guard.

Why had she not taken the time to find the keys to the smuggling organization? Had that been a mistake? It probably *had* been. Had she taken that time before now, it was possible that she would have known who this was, so that she wouldn't have to move blindly through the city. Now she felt as if she were wasting time, time that was precious to her, time that was key to finding out who had harmed her friend, and who still posed a risk to the city.

Someone had hired an assassin.

Her mind continued to race through what she'd heard. He had said that he had his target. *Lindy* had been his target. But why?

The only thing she could she could think of was that Lindy had been targeted because she was felt to be the key to Carth's network in the city. They had made no effort to conceal Lindy's role. She had played a prominent part in the city, serving as the person who ran their network, and Lindy had been instrumental in organizing not only the hospital, but also the connection between the taverns. Someone in the city resented that, and had intended to take it out.

Had they known about Carth's role?

Neither of them had made an effort to conceal Carth's responsibility. She had always been a part of the running of the network, though Carth preferred to work from the fringes, not to be front and center, which was why she had allowed Lindy to take such a prominent role. It was the same reason she had installed Dara in Reva.

But now, Carth was forced to take a prominent role in Asador. With Lindy's passing, women looked to her. Carth couldn't ignore that responsibility, just as she couldn't ignore the murder of her friend. She would find out what happened, and she would have answers.

The man turned down a side street towards the center of the city, and some of the more prominent tradesmen. Asador was unique in that it had a council comprised of tradesmen as well as elected officials; there was no singular rule for the city. Because of that, each area had its own distinct needs, and issues. Those issues often were different from place to place, enough so that conflict occasionally occurred.

The man glanced around him before hurrying on.

Carth smiled tightly to herself. She maintained her connection to the shadows, remaining hidden within them. The shadows, and this time of day, were hers. She could stay hidden in the darkness, could stay hidden in the night, and no one would ever know she was there. There was power in that. The only people who recognized her presence had been another shadow blessed and the assassin. Even those of Lashasn didn't have the same ability to detect when she moved within the shadows.

Carth followed him as he entered a shop.

She paused at the door, scanning the street and finding it otherwise empty. This was a blacksmith shop, and a prominent one by the looks of the sign. The shop was well built and freshly painted, and had a clear glass window in front, inviting shoppers in.

On either side of the blacksmith were other similar

merchants. On one side was a metalsmith, one with exquisite jewelry. On the other was a fletcher, likely someone who worked with the blacksmith.

She trailed the man as he went through the back of the shop and through another door, and Carth realized that it connected on the other side to another building.

It reminded her all too much of the interconnectedness that she'd discovered in Hoga's shop. There had been similar connected buildings when she had searched for her friends after they been captured. Was all of Asador connected like this?

Carth moved more carefully now. With the shadows around her, she worried that it would appear more like an inky fog. She had to be careful that she didn't reveal herself. She didn't want the smuggler, or whoever he worked with, to recognize her presence.

She was in a large room, empty other than a few long benches. They were angled together, looking like a meeting had recently been held here. The hearth in the corner of the room still held the occasional glowing ember. The air smelled of smoke, but of something else too, a familiar sweet scent that reminded her of the perfume Lindy had preferred. The memory made her heart lurch, thinking of what had happened to her friend.

The man had gone through a door on the opposite side. Carth followed, and when the door opened up, he was gone.

How had she lost him? How many disappeared so quickly from her?

Better yet, how had he recognized that she'd trailed him?

Carth stood on the street, scanning in every direction, hopeful that she would find him once more, but he had truly disappeared.

She swore to herself and, pulling on the shadows, she jumped to the next rooftop.

CHAPTER 14

CARTH CLUTCHED A PAIR OF THE POISONED BLADES IN her hand, holding them by the tips, ready to throw them were she to come across any of the smugglers. They seemed to know that she was there and to be prepared for her, although Carth didn't know why that should be.

How were they able to detect her presence?

She moved silently, holding on to the shadows as she did, barely making any sound.

The darkness fit her mood and her mindset. She had felt nothing but darkness in the days since losing Lindy.

She followed the smuggler more closely than she had the last few. She wasn't about to lose track of him, not like she had the others. There had been two nights when she had followed smugglers, and both times they had disappeared before she'd managed to find out who they were meeting with. She'd grown increasingly frustrated by that. There had to be something about the smugglers she'd missed. Either they recognized that she was there, or they were disappearing someplace else. Using her magics, she hadn't been able to find out where they disappeared to.

This time, Carth was determined not to let this man escape from her. When she saw him pushing his carts from the docks, she jumped on the roof of the building, landing in front of him.

She jabbed up with her knife, practically piercing the underside of his neck. If she were to break the skin, poison would flow. She didn't have narcass to reverse the effect. She wasn't sure she was interested in reversing it anyway.

"You're going to take me to your organization."

The man's eyes drifted to the knife before darting up to her face. He nervously licked his lips. "You can have it."

Carth shook her head. "I think you misunderstand me. I don't want what's in your cart. I want to know where the others are. I need to meet the man who leads you."

"I can't. They'll kill me."

Carth twisted the knife. It was barely beneath the

surface of the skin. She surged a hint of the flame through it, enough that he could feel the heat from the blade.

It was effective. He jerked his head back.

"What makes you think that I won't kill you?"

His eyes widened. "You don't understand," he started.

"Perhaps I don't. Which is why you're going to take me where I tell you. Then I'm going to have a little conversation with your boss."

The man's gaze shot to the knife again before turning back to her. He licked his lips again and finally nodded.

Carth pulled the knife back only a little, but held it out, keeping it close to him. The smuggler would not escape her. Unfortunately, there was no way to keep her presence hidden. Not only would they know she was here, Carth meant to find the key to the smuggling ring. If she didn't play this the right way, she envisioned others armed and opposing her—and the women who worked with her.

The man weaved through the city, still pushing his cart, his back stiff as he made his way along the streets. Carth noted he went in a different direction than the previous two had. The first man had gone to typical traders, then disappeared somewhere around the blacksmith shop. The second man had gone along the shore, making her think that there was perhaps another place he might've hidden, one similar to what Guya had done when smuggling women out of the city before disappearing.

This man headed south.

South of the city, the streets began sloping downward. Carth hadn't spent much time exploring the side, but knew that it headed inland, toward the flat plains outside of the city. Shops began to dwindle, giving way to small houses. The entire streetscape was dingier, and she wondered where he brought her.

He moved quickly and with purpose. When he stopped at a house with a plain wooden door, Carth studied it before noting that it was connected to several others. Everything was darkened around her, and if not for her connection to the shadows, she doubted she'd be able to see much.

He pushed the door open, sliding his cart inside, and waited.

Would he try to bolt? He made no effort to try to escape. Instead, he waited, seeming to know that she could reach him were she to want to.

When she stepped inside, she noted a hint of pine in the air. It covered another scent, one that reminded her of the hospital. It was the same kind of scent that reminded her of Alex's shop, that of different powders and leaves and other plants.

Carth looked over to the smuggler. "Here? You're bringing me here?"

"This is the place. I tell you—"

Carth pointed the knife at him. She didn't really want to use the knife, but she needed to know whether he was leading her astray.

"I've followed several others. Some of them ended up in other parts of the city than this. Why here?"

The man shook his head. "Come with me. You'll see."

He left the cart in the entryway of the room and moved through the building. Carth followed him until he reached a doorway with stairs leading down.

Carth frowned. Was this why she hadn't found the others? They'd gone beneath the street level?

Another doorway to the bottom of the stairs, and he pulled it open. A long tunnel stretched into the darkness. With sudden understanding, Carth realized that this must be the same set of tunnels Alex's building rested on. It was the same set of tunnels that had been beneath Hoga's building. Those tunnels connected beneath the city.

Carth felt her heart racing. Was this going to be the same as what she had discovered before? Was she going to find women chained to the wall with an intent to smuggle them out of the city much as Guya had done?

She wasn't prepared for that kind of fight, but she

would have to be. If women were trapped, they deserved that from her.

The man started down the tunnels, and she followed him. The ceiling arched over her head, reaching several feet above her, enough that she couldn't easily touch it. The tunnels had been made for someone much taller than her. Carth was of average height, and so was the smuggler, as well as most of the people of Asador. Only a few people were much taller than that. The green-eyed man who had attacked her was much taller. The man who led the Hjan had also been tall.

Carth hesitated. She'd been working under the belief that the man had been after her because of her desire to break up the smuggling ring, but what if that weren't the case? What if she had been attacked because he worked for the Hjan?

If so, that meant they'd violated the accords.

Carth doubted they were interested in that. For now, they were interested in the protection, but it was possible that something had changed that she didn't fully understand.

They continued along the Hall, and Carth noted doors leading off. They were connected, likely to places overhead. Now she understood why other smugglers she had followed had disappeared. They had all come here, only they had followed a different pathway to these tunnels.

There was a certain sort of sense about such a plan. Using the tunnels, having people enter from different directions, took attention off them. She could imagine how easy it would be to track some of the smugglers if they all used the same entrance, or even if they came to the same section of the city. Finding buildings like this to reach this network of tunnels would keep the attention from them.

The tunnel began to widen as they went. More doorways lined the tunnel, with likely more buildings entering here. There was a look of activity here, the stone heavily trampled, and bits of debris dropped along the corridor. This was a place others frequented.

The long hall ended in a section of what appeared to be a blank stone wall, mortar cracked in places, and some of the stone crumbling. There was moisture damage to the wall as well, water seeping from the stones, trailing down to the ground.

Carth watched the smuggler, curious what he might do here, and he tapped a series of stones. When he did, there was a soft rumbling, and then a section of the wall pulled away.

Had Carth not been with the smuggler—had she not forced him to bring her—there wouldn't have been any way she would have known how to open the section of wall. Even were she to reach the tunnels—which she thought she could, especially accessing them by Alex's shop—she would never have known about another room on the other side of the wall.

As the wall slid away, light spilled out. The smuggler led her through it, and pressed on another set of stones on the other side, letting the wall slide back into place.

Once done, he looked over at Carth, concern plain on his face, before nodding to the rest of the room.

Carth surveyed the room. This was a more ornate area. A massive staircase with a wide banister led down, made of some dark metal. The flooring here was planked wood over the stone, giving it a more formal air. Paintings hung along the wall, as if this were an entry parlor.

"Down the stairs. That's where you need to go," he said.

"You're going to take me there."

The smuggler shook his head. "Please. Don't make me."

Carth surged the A'ras magic through her knife, sending heat through it. He took a step back. Briefly, she wondered whether the heat damaged this knife, or damaged the poison on the blade. It was something she hadn't a chance to test.

"Fine."

The smuggler reached the stairs and led her down them slowly, his head bowed as he did. She followed behind him, prepared with both the shadows and flame for whatever she might encounter.

At the bottom of the stairs, Carth stopped. Bright light illuminated the room. It was paneled entirely in wood. The floor was planked and a plush carpet was rolled across it. Flames crackled along one wall, leaving a hint of smoke drifting in the room, but otherwise the room was well ventilated, the smoke blowing out of the room somewhere high overhead.

Carth's eyes were drawn toward the people in the room. Rows of tables with benches and chairs filled the room. Others sat at the tables—men she'd seen at the docks—making her realize this was a smugglers' hole. Most sat quietly, eating and drinking, though some played games of dice and others played a board game that reminded her of Tsatsun.

It was a tavern.

"This is where you brought me?" Carth asked.

"You wanted to see the leader. This is where you have to find her."

As Carth stared around the room, a comment sank in. She turned her attention back to the smuggler, a smile crossing her face. "Her?"

The smuggler nodded.

Interesting. Carth hadn't expected the leader of the smugglers guild to be a woman. Maybe they would be able to find some common ground.

She took a seat at a table, and a waiter hurried over, bringing two mugs of ale. "What's your name?"

The man looked around him before sighing. "Ronald."

He took a long drink of his ale, though Carth ignored hers. Every so often, he cast a furtive glance around the tavern.

Carth found herself looking with him. Would she see the woman who ran this tavern? So far, all she saw were men. Even the server—a man with a gray apron tied tightly around him, his belly protruding beneath it —had been a man.

Her gaze drifted back to him, and she noted him watching, his hands clasped over his belly as he watched her with a strange expression on his face.

It took Carth a moment to realize why. She was the only woman in the tavern.

Others made a point of not looking at her, though she sensed their attention and knew that they were fully aware of her presence. Carth smiled inwardly. This was nothing like what she had expected.

"Where is she?" Carth asked.

"She'll come to you. Once she hears that you're here, she'll come."

They waited. She had questions. Many questions. Was this woman responsible for attacking those Carth cared about? If she wasn't, maybe she knew who had been.

Given the numbers in the tavern, she doubted she would easily be able to fight her way free were it necessary. And if she did, she didn't know if she would be able to find her way back through that brick doorway. She didn't remember the combination of stones to press to open it.

She sat, prepared for whatever might come, and waited.

Eventually, a door opened on the other wall, and a woman entered who caused Carth's breath to catch.

She had dark hair, pale skin, and deep brown eyes. She had a certain sway to her walk, one that practically dared the men sitting around the tavern not to look.

"Lindy," Carth breathed out.

The woman looked just like Lindy, as if finding her perfect twin.

The woman scanned the tavern, a hard edge to her eyes before they settled on Ronald and then Carth. She offered a half smile as she meandered through the tavern, stopping several of the tables before making her way over to Carth. When she stopped, her demeanor changed. Her hint of a smile faded, replaced by a sudden sternness. Her body was tensed, coiled like a snake as it readied to strike. Carth noticed a slight bulge beneath her dress, and realized that she was armed as well.

"You aren't meant to be here," the woman said.

Carth sat up, leaving her mug of ale untouched. "No? And where am I supposed to be?"

The woman turned to Ronald. "What were you thinking, bringing her down here?"

Ronald's eyes widened. "I was thinking I didn't want to die."

The woman harrumphed. "You worry more about her than me?"

"She was the one with the knife."

With a flourish so quick that Carth almost didn't see it, the woman brandished a pair of knives in front of her. They were of a different make than the poisoned blade Carth had. There was a dull sheen to them, but the edge was sharp.

"I have a knife as well," the woman said.

"Come on, Marna. I didn't have much of a choice. Didn't you tell us to do what was necessary?"

Marna's eyes narrowed slightly and she laughed. She might look like Lindy, but her manner of speaking and the edge to her were nothing like Lindy. This was a woman used to being in charge. This was a woman used to being obeyed. Lindy had struggled with running the hospital, struggled with her growing responsibilities within the city.

Marna waved at Ronald. "You can go. I think I will sit and talk with your friend here."

Ronald glanced to Carth, and she realized that he waited for her to give him permission. She nodded once, and a relieved expression crossed his face. He hurriedly stood, pushing the stool back so quickly that it started to tip, forcing him to grab it.

Marna got to it first. She snatched the falling stool, righting it, and then sat upon it just as quickly. Carth barely had time to react before Marna was seated across from her.

This was not just a woman accustomed to being obeyed. This was a dangerous woman.

"So. You wanted to find me."

"You don't seem terribly surprised to see me here."

"Why should I be surprised to see you? You've been busy organizing everyone up there. Truth be told, I was expecting to see you long ago."

Carth glanced around the tavern. "You're responsible for this?"

"If you mean this place, organizing these idiots into something more cohesive, then yes. If you mean something else, then I'd ask you to explain."

"You know women are being attacked?" Carth had a suspicion that Marna was quite aware of what took place in her city. A part of her wanted Marna to admit that.

"The attacks. Yes. An unfortunate thing. It's a good thing you were there to protect those people."

Carth shook her head. "I couldn't protect all of them."

"Neither could I."

"Who have you lost?" Carth asked.

Marna considered her, her gaze unsettling. "What happened? Did you lose someone you cared about?"

Carth nodded.

Marna leaned forward. "And you think that perhaps I have something to do with this?"

"I thought that you might."

Now Carth wasn't sure. The assassin had been looking for a woman like Lindy, and Carth assumed she'd been the target. But what if the assassin had sought Marna?

Carth's gaze drifted around the tavern and she began to have a different realization.

Was this where Marna had hidden?

"You knew," Carth said.

The pieces started to come together, like a game falling into place for her. Her heart started to thunder in her chest, and she knew that she was right. She could play the pieces out, moving them in such a way that she would see how Marna had used the similarity between her and Lindy to her advantage.

Marna had known she was hunted and had hidden here, staying protected from whoever the assassin was.

"Do you know who it was?" Carth asked.

Marna stared at her blankly. "I thought perhaps you might be angrier that I used your friend."

Carth clenched her jaw. She was angry enough, but

she wouldn't let Marna see it. All of this had to be part of her game. "I want vengeance. That's all."

"Then you're a fool. I thought the shadow walker was cleverer than that. Perhaps those rumors were wrong?"

Carth resisted the urge to grab her hidden knife. A part of her wanted to take it, stab it into Marna's chest, but it wouldn't bring Lindy back. It wouldn't bring the vengeance she sought. She needed to control her emotions, control that had not been difficult until recently. For some reason, losing Lindy had changed that for her.

"What do you know?"

"Nothing that will bring you the answers you seek," Marna said. "Nothing that will bring your friend back."

Carth fixed her with a hard stare. "I need answers. If it involves me tearing through your entire network to get them, I will do so. Don't think me helpless."

Marna flourished her knives so quickly that Carth could barely see them, slamming them into the table on either side of Carth's arms, creating a cage. "And don't think me helpless either."

Marna sat back, crossing her arms and leaving the knives in place as an unspoken threat. "I'm sorry I can't be of any more help to you. I thought it best to allow you to make your way here, show you that there is little you can do at this point. And again, I'm truly sorry about your friend, but this way, others won't suffer."

"They'll learn that you still live."

"Will they? I think rumor of a greater threat will reach them." Marna stared for a long moment and then stood from the table, leaving Carth alone, the pint of ale in front of her untouched.

Carth realized that she had been well and thoroughly played, without even realizing that it had been a game.

CHAPTER 15

Carth made her way into the hospital. Her mind raced with what she'd seen of the underground tavern. Somehow, Marna had used her.

No... she hadn't used Carth, she had used Lindy. She had sacrificed Lindy so that Marna could survive, so that Marna wouldn't be attacked by this assassin and whoever had hired him.

Evie caught her at the door and turned to her. "What is it?"

Carth gripped her knife, sending shadows swirling around it. She had only vaguely remembered unsheathing her knife, barely recalling pulling it out. "I know a little bit more about why Lindy died."

"You learned who hired the sellsword?"

Carth frowned. "Sellsword?"

Evie shrugged. "Assassin. Sellsword. Whatever you want to call it. If we knew the poison…"

"I thought Alex knew what was used."

"She thought so too. Now she's not quite sure."

Carth scanned the hospital. The cots were empty today, the people who'd died over the last few weeks long since burned, and those who had been injured now recovered. She should be pleased by that fact, but it troubled her that so many had to lose because of the smuggling in the city. Worse, for it to end, she needed the help of someone who could manage the city, to bring the fighting to an end. This was not something she could do herself. She needed Lindy.

"Jamie and Alice left today," Evie said.

Carth sighed. At least there was that. Having recovered—even if it was an injury that had come by her hand—and foot—meant something. They could get married, live their lives.

"Where did they go?" Carth asked.

"Out of the city. She wanted to get away from here. And he… he wanted nothing to do with us."

"How certain are you that this was a sellsword?" Carth asked. She thought of Timothy, and how he'd been hired to abduct her, though in reality he had a different task. There were others like him, others with a similar skill set. Before Lindy had died, she'd even considered going to him for help.

"I don't know. There are many known to use

poisons. If we could be certain what poison *had* been used, it might make it easier to find, but…"

Alex had thought she'd known the poison, but was no longer certain. Now Carth had to figure out which it was. Once she did, then they could search for who had used it.

Carth looked around the hospital. What would she do now? Without Lindy, she didn't know where she would go, who she would coordinate her movements with, none of it.

She felt lost without her friend.

Yet… she shouldn't. Planning and strategy were what she was good at, though connecting to the local resources was something she *wasn't* always good at. It was the reason she had left Dara in Reva. It was the reason Lindy had been successful here. Now she would have to figure out how to connect to those who were left behind in the city.

The network was hers. There had been no doubting the fact that she was responsible for coordinating it. It would take time, and it would take her remaining more actively involved, but was that the best use of her time?

She turned back to the door, looking away from Evie. As she turned to leave, Evie spoke up. "Where are you going to go?"

"I need to get a few more answers before I can decide."

"What kind of answers?"

Carth thought about her response. What would she do? Should she stay in the city? Or should she continue to attack, going after the assassin who had killed Lindy?

Maybe the right answer was a combination. It was one that she would have to take some time to determine, but she would have to act.

Daylight shone on the deck of the *Goth Spald*, dispersing any shadows Carth could use. There were hints of them, especially around the mast, and down underneath the deck of the ship, but they weren't easily accessible. It wasn't that Carth couldn't use shadows in the daytime, only that she had less strength with them, and less potential. It forced her to rely on the power of the flame.

Carth tapped her foot as she waited. The salt breeze blew in from the north, carrying with it a hint of a chill. It was almost enough to make her think longingly back to her time in Nyaesh. That was a time when Lindy had still been alive.

She waited, knowing that there was only so much time she could wait. She had to know, though. Before she made a decision, she had to know.

Movement along the street caught her attention. Carth used the power of her flame magic, helping her pick out the distinct signature of Alex making her way towards the ship. When she reached the dock, Carth met her as she came up the ramp. Alex carried a heavy satchel with her, and a sheen of sweat glistened on her cheeks.

"I brought you all the different poisons I can think of." Alex set the satchel down and crossed her arms over her chest. "I still don't think that's safe for you."

"It wasn't terad," Carth said. "It was my mistake, we had prepared as if it was terad. We'd been using the narcass leaves thinking that they would protect us. But it was not terad."

"I warned you that you should have given me a chance to figure out what we were dealing with. Going in without knowing… that put you in danger. That put her in danger."

"I discovered the reason why Lindy was targeted. There was a woman in the underground. Marna—"

"Marna?" Alex asked quickly. Her breath caught, and she shook her head. "If Marna was involved, we need to be careful."

"You know about her?"

"I've heard the name. It's hard to get anybody who knows Marna. She keeps herself hidden, protected."

"Why haven't you told me about her?" Carth asked. "Why hide it from me?"

"Because she's dangerous, Carth. She runs the smugglers in a way…"

"In what way?"

"In the way that you would like to run your network. If you go after her, be careful."

Carth intended to be careful, but she would discover what secrets Marna kept from her.

CHAPTER 16

THE POISON DRIPPED DOWN THE BACK OF HER THROAT, leaving her skin burning, the sensation that of fire racing through her. Carth allowed the poison to seep into her, letting the awareness of it surge until it became unbearable. Only then did she reach for the power of the flame and shadows to burn it off.

Alex watched her from behind the counter in the herbalist shop, her eyes narrowed and a worried expression furrowing her brow. She said nothing, having long since shared her concern about Carth's plan to test every poison that she could. What more could Alex say that would deter her? Carth needed to know what poison had been used, so that she could determine who was to blame for the killings.

Sweat beaded up on her brow, and she wiped it away, smearing it across her forehead.

Her legs buckled, but she stabilized herself, drawing on the strength of the shadows to keep standing. It wouldn't do for her to allow Alex to see how weak the poison made her. The woman might refuse to provide her with others, and Carth was determined to know exactly *what* poison had been used.

"It feels like fire," she said through gritted teeth. As much as she might want to hide the effects of the poison, there was nothing she could truly do to ignore them completely. Allowing herself to feel the poison as it worked through her, to experience what others would have experienced, made that impossible, and Carth was determined to know the way the poisoning felt, to feel it as it incapacitated her. "My skin. My insides. My blood."

As she said the last, she sent another surge of the flame magic through her. It was a cleansing sense, one that heated everything inside of her, scorching away the effects of the poison. So far, she hadn't encountered a poison that she couldn't eliminate, but she knew they existed. Facing Hoga had demonstrated that there were particular poisons that she couldn't counter. That was why Alex was here. If it came to it, the herbalist could dose her with narcass or with any of the other antidotes she possessed. It wasn't ideal, but what choice did she have? She needed answers.

"Srirach," Alex said with a nod. She started toward one of her shelves, pulled out a vial of reddish powder, and tipped a small amount onto the counter. The light caught it in such a way that the powder appeared to sparkle, going from a deep red to almost purple. "One of the worst ways to go, from what I hear. For most, the burning persists until you can't stand it anymore and pass out from the pain. It's a lingering sort of death. Horrible, really."

Carth licked her lips. It was unpleasant, but then, she had the advantage that she knew how to counter it and didn't have to subject herself to the ongoing misery of the poison. Not like others would have. They would continue to suffer, and would continue to face the fiery torment racing through their veins.

"It's not srirach."

"Not from what you've described," Alex agreed. She wiped the powder off the counter and replaced the jar of srirach on the shelf before taking out another.

"Why do you have it on the shelves if it's such a violent way to go?" Carth asked.

"There are other uses for srirach," Alex said. "Not everything that can kill is meant for killing. Think of your knives," she said, nodding to the pair of knives sheathed at Carth's waist. "Do you think they're only meant for killing? Can't they be used to cut your food, or to help with the lines on the ship, or—"

"These aren't meant for anything so practical," Carth said. "Sometimes things are weapons."

Alex shrugged. "And sometimes they're tools.

Dangerous tools, to be sure, but tools just the same. Now, try this one." She placed a small amount of pale white powder into a bowl.

Carth stared at the powder. This would be the fifth poison that she intended to try, and so far, she'd come no closer to knowing what the assassin had used on his blade, no closer to understanding the way that Lindy had died. She was determined to discover that secret, if only so she could know *who* to target.

She had to find the answer. For Lindy, she had to.

Carth dipped a finger into the powder and brought it to her lips.

It had a bitter taste and made her lips numb immediately. Her tongue followed, and she found that everything the powder touched went numb. As it hit her stomach, she struggled to breathe. With a panicked surge of the shadows, she drew power, then sent the A'ras flame magic through her, destroying the traces of the poison.

"What about that one?" Alex asked.

"That… that was unpleasant," Carth said. In some ways, it was worse than the srirach. At least with the srirach, you could feel the way the poison burned, and you had time to attempt to counter it, even if that was unlikely. With this, the numbness washed through her so quickly that, without her abilities, she doubted she would be able to do anything to stop the effects. "My mouth, my throat, went numb. It became hard to breathe."

"Ylish powder. Some call it by other names, but it's the one I know. It's effective for stitching wounds. Dust a little on the wound and it goes numb. Hard to find, so there aren't many healers who use it, but when you do…"

"If it's used like that, why did you let me try it as a poison?"

Alex placed the jar of ylish powder back beneath the counter. "Because as I said, not everything that's used as a poison is *meant* as a poison. Even too much water can kill, Carth."

She smiled, trying to think of someone dying from water. "Too much water?"

Alex nodded. "I've seen men mad from the sea, thinking they're thirsty, and they drink so much water that they die. It's awful in its own way. Ylish powder is an effective anesthetic, but when you swallow it… then it becomes something different."

The woman's knowledge continued to impress Carth. Not only did she have the necessary connections within the city to find these powders, but she had the knowledge to use them. She was more knowledgeable than Carth's mother had been, and she had seemed to know quite a bit about plants and their uses. Then again, Hoga had a terrifying knowledge of plants and their uses, and had managed to find ways to combine them to counter the effect of different magics. They still used some of that knowledge, but they'd lost something with Hoga's disappearance that they still hadn't regained.

Alex reached for another jar, this time one with a thick oil in it. She spooned out a small amount and then mixed a grayish powder into it. The combination turned a faint blue, one that practically seemed to glow.

"What is this one?" Carth asked.

Alex shook her head. "You need to try it first. This would be rarer than some of the others, mostly because there probably aren't too many who have the patience to mix the olinph oil. That can take days, and even one wrong stir can leave the entire batch destroyed."

"I'm beginning to think that you are more dangerous than you let on," Carth said.

"Me? I know enough to be dangerous, but Hoga was the one who really knew these compounds. A shame she's disappeared."

"A shame," Carth agreed. A woman like her wouldn't stay hidden for long, and there was the matter of the different plants she needed to find to make her concoctions work. Carth had limited the supply out of Asador, but that did nothing to prevent her from going elsewhere, to any of the great cities along the coast or even inland. She could even have gone across the sea. With Guya, Hoga would have connections to the smugglers. If she ever determined who ran them, she would see if that was information they possessed.

"Try this. I warn you, the combination is unique."

Carth glanced to Alex, and then dipped her finger into the liquid. It was sticky and left her finger burning, but not in the same way that the srirach had. Carth brought the liquid to her lips, ready for the same sort of numbness that she'd experienced from the last, but there was none of it. It tasted sweet, with an undertone of something harsher, and she licked the liquid off her lips.

Immediately, all strength in her body failed.

She dropped to the ground, unable to hold herself up.

Carth tried moving her arms, but they didn't respond. Her mouth wouldn't even open for her to take a breath. She would suffocate, and in a different way than with the terad they had been experimenting on.

Panic raced through her, and she had to force her mind to slow so that she could focus on reaching for her abilities. The flame magic eluded her, and the shadows… they were there, but just beyond her grasp. She could detect the shadows, but they slipped away from her.

She couldn't breathe. The poison suffocated her, and now, there was a hint of something more, visions of those she'd known and failed, that came to her.

"Carth?"

She heard Alex's voice as a distant sound, almost a memory.

Had the woman done this to her intentionally?

No, she had been trying to help Carth, and she had warned her against trying the poisons, as if she had known what Carth might come across.

She felt something on her arm, and she shuddered. Was this the blood priests coming to take her away? Was this the Hjan?

Her heart hammered, and she could feel it as it seemed like it wanted to leap from her chest. It was the only thing she was really aware of.

Then her head was tipped back. Something was poured into her mouth and she was forced to swallow.

More poison.

Alex *was* trying to kill her.

She couldn't even reach for her knives. Maybe this had been the intent. She had wanted to gain Carth's trust long enough for her to be able to poison her.

As she swallowed, feeling returned to her arms, and then her legs. She was able to breathe.

The terror that she'd been feeling began to abate, but didn't disappear completely. It was still there, but more as a vague sense of unease.

"Carth?" Alex asked.

Carth opened her eyes, realizing that they had been closed through the ordeal. "What happened?"

Alex held a small clear vial in her hand and her eyes

were wide. "You were... shouting."

"Shouting? I couldn't move."

Alex shook her head. "That's the effect of this. It forces your fears forward and immobilizes you, but you still *can* move. As I said, this one is interesting."

"I couldn't use my abilities."

"You could," Alex said.

Carth shook her head. "I couldn't. I tried, but they eluded me."

"You only thought that they did. They were there. You were... glowing... with power. And shadows swirled around you. I wasn't sure you were going to let me get close enough to help you. I thought that maybe you would..."

"Ignite you?"

Alex nodded. "Something like that. When I saw you weren't going to get past it on your own, I risked it to give you the antidote." Alex sat back and studied her. "We can stop for now. You don't need to keep at it."

Carth shook her head. She did. She needed to know what poison had been used. "We keep at it," she said. She would do it for Lindy.

"If only we knew where Hoga had gone."

Carth snorted. It was something *she* should have thought of. "Maybe we can find her."

"How?"

"I think it's time we draw her out." And Carth knew how she would do it.

CHAPTER 17

CARTH RACED THROUGH THE STREETS OF ASADOR, STILL feeling some of the effects of the last poison she'd attempted to use. After meeting with Alex, it was clear that what she needed now was to find Hoga. The woman was going to be key to helping her understand the poison that had been used, and who might have been responsible. There was only one other person in the city that she thought might be able to help her, but Carth was uncertain whether Marna would be willing.

She didn't intend to give her much of a choice.

The woman had been responsible for what had happened to Lindy, and Carth would see her avenged. That required that Marna would help her.

Only Carth somehow had to reach her.

The woman kept herself isolated. Carth had monitored the various entrances to the underground tunnel network and had so far never seen her make an appearance. Carth had tasked the women who worked with her with looking for Marna as well, and they hadn't found anything. Given the nature of Marna's business, the fact that she smuggled and needed to keep it away from the city council, she suspected that she would be difficult to reach. But Carth was determined to find her.

Even if it meant drawing her out.

And that was what she intended to do now.

Carth tracked a smuggler as he made his way towards the tunnel entrance. Using one of the sedatives that Alex had taught her, she crept up to him and dosed him with a syringe filled with it. It was just enough to sedate him, barely more than a few drops, the rest of it diluted with water. It was enough to be effective, though.

The man crumpled, and she motioned to two of her women waiting in the shadows. They raced out and grabbed him, and Carth took his cart, hurrying along the street with it. Whatever else happened, Carth was determined to find a way to pull Marna out of hiding.

Carth hurried through the street with the cart. The other women would carry the smuggler back to the hospital, where they had retrofitted it into a sort of cell. She hadn't wanted to begin a battle for control of the city, but it seemed Marna was going to force her. And while Marna might know the underground connections better than Carth, Carth knew the streets, and she knew the rooftops.

Carth loaded the contents of the smuggler onto her ship. The *Goth Spald* was a trading ship and had plenty of room for in the hold for everything she might find. She didn't expect to need to reach too much before Marna reacted. And she didn't intend to kill anyone. This was all part of her plan to draw her out. That was all she wanted—all she needed. She could do that, she could coax Marna aboveground, and possibly to a meeting. Then she would find out the information she needed. Then she would use Marna to find Hoga.

Carth waited in the hold of the ship. There were more supplies now than there'd ever been when she'd traveled with Guya. Between chasing after the smugglers and sedating and capturing over a dozen, she had now collected enough goods to fill about a quarter of the ship's hold. Some of the items here were odd. Carth noted some jewels that would have some value on the open market. In addition to the jewels, some of the smugglers had different spices and powders, all of which she had had Alex evaluate. Most of them had some innate value, while others had value simply because they were difficult to prepare, but all of them came from somewhere outside of the city.

She noted knives in one basket that had contained several swords. Carth had claimed one of them for herself. She'd needed a sword since coming to Asador, and rather than waiting for a metalsmith to forge her one, she would just confiscate this one. The sword had a nice heft to it, and it was well-balanced.

In her time studying in Nyaesh, she had grown comfortable gauging the quality of swords. This particular blade had been finely made. It was plain otherwise, not as ornate as some of the other swords the smugglers had been moving, but with the quality of the blade, she suspected they knew what they were getting.

Carth was holding on to her sense of the shadows, as well as the flame, when she detected movement outside the ship.

It was not the kind of movement that came from any of the women working with her. Plenty of those women knew about the *Goth Spald*—it was not necessarily a secret, but few were willing to come onto her ship, wanting her permission first.

The sense came from somebody already on the deck of the ship.

When Lindy had lived, Carth would have expected her to have joined her on the ship. When Dara was still in town, she would have visited. Alex had visited her on the ship as well, but only when Carth had invited her. This was none of them.

And yet, it was not an unfamiliar person.

Carth had detected this signature before.

She smiled.

Had Marna thought to surprise her by coming onto her ship?

If she had, Carth would prove that she wouldn't be so easily surprised the second time.

Slipping up a back staircase to the deck, she poked her head out, peering into the shadows. Carth drew upon the shadows, using them, and saw Marna as well as two men with her. They were looking toward the back railing of the ship, hidden in the shadows, but not hidden from Carth.

Carth pulled upon the strength of her shadow power, using it to surge her body upward, and practically soared into the air, flying above the deck, where she reached the mast. Carth clung to it, wondering if she'd made too much noise. She never practiced this maneuver before, but she could hang from here, use this place to hide, remain separate from those on the deck of her ship.

Carth cloaked herself in the shadows, hiding within them.

"She's not here. We've not seen anyone moving on or off the ship for the last day." This came from one of the men with Marna.

Carth smiled to herself.

They believed they were protected because they hadn't seen her moving on or off the ship?

She slid down the mast, dropping slowly, going hand over hand, carefully, so that she didn't alert them to her presence. She wanted to get closer, so that she could not only listen but could also hear what they were doing, and she could be ready to attack them if it came to it.

"I've been warned not to underestimate her," Marna said.

Carth hesitated. Warned? That made it sound as if Marna worked with someone else. She'd thought Marna ran the smuggling ring, but maybe that wasn't the case. Maybe there was somebody else who was involved.

"Anything they would've taken would be in the hold."

"Just find it. It was bad enough when she started attacking, but now she's managed to get something I actually need."

"She probably doesn't even know what she has."

"No. I doubt that she does. I think it angered her that she lost someone she cared about. She thinks that if she takes those who work with me, I'll be equally angered."

Carth smiled to herself. They thought her more impulsive than she was. If her training had taught her nothing else, it was that acting impulsively was a mistake. She couldn't risk acting like that, not if she intended to be successful with her plans. Even in revenge, she would act thoughtfully.

Carth wondered what it was that she possessed that had driven Marna onto the ship. This was a woman who had played Carth, who had used someone she'd cared about in such a way that she could eliminate a threat to herself. This was a calculating woman, and Carth needed to be equally calculating. Whatever it was she intended, Carth had to not only discover it but prevent her from doing it.

An idea came to her.

Sliding a little further down the mast, she reached the railing where the ship was tied and sliced through the rope before crawling along the railing and reaching the rope at the back. Once there, she sliced the rear line, and then, surging on the shadows, she pushed the ship away from the dock.

It moved slowly at first, but with Carth massaging her connection to the shadows, she sent them out to sea. The ship picked up speed, and Carth continued to pull on the shadows, thankful they'd been foolish enough to come at night, when her connection to the shadows was strongest. She could use the shadows, and she did, sending the ship deeper into the sea. By the time they noticed the ship was moving, it was already too late.

The water here was deep enough that swimming back to shore would be difficult, even if they could swim. Only then did Carth jump to the deck, making her presence known. Carth released her connection to the shadows, maintaining some sense of them, as well as a sense of the flame.

Doing so revealed her to the two men, but Marna was the only one that Carth cared about.

"That's how you want this to be?" Marna asked.

"I think I want some answers from you. I didn't expect it to be quite this way, but this will work," Carth said.

"You are one person on a ship with three," Marna said. "Even with the abilities that I've seen you possess, I don't think you will be able to get off the ship safely."

Carth watched Marna. The woman had skill, and speed, something that Carth could counter with her abilities, if she was ready. Now that she had seen it, now that she knew what to expect, she was prepared for her. At the same time, Carth had begun to suspect that whatever Marna possessed was not necessarily an inborn talent, not quite like Carth's shadow ability or her ability to use the flame. Whatever it was reminded her more of the concoctions Alex mixed, making her think that it was something like Hoga's medicines and augmentations.

Perhaps she worked with Hoga.

That would make it easier for her to find Hoga for Carth.

"I see two men with you, and yourself," Carth said

with a shrug. As she did, she pulled needles from her pocket that Alex had prepared. Both were filled with a sedative, something Alex had referred to as coxberry. It was a strange substance, one that led to sedation, but nothing more. It was painless, and Carth had taken it often enough in the weeks since Alex had introduced her to it that she had built up a tolerance to it even without using her own magical ability. Would these men have a similar resistance?

Carth didn't think they would, but was prepared if they did. She had used a double dose, twice what Alex normally recommended. She flung the darts at the men, using a hint of shadow to make sure they flew true. When the needles sunk into the men's necks, they staggered a moment before falling.

Marna gave a casual glance to her now-fallen soldiers. "That was impressive. Unexpected as well. Now… you have only me to deal with. Is that what you wanted?"

Carth shrugged. "I didn't want to attack you, if that's what you're thinking. As I said, I want vengeance for what happened to my friend. That doesn't necessarily mean killing you."

Marna's eyes widened the slightest amount. Carth could almost see the woman's calculating mind working through what Carth had shared. Under different circumstances, Carth thought Marna might be an interesting person to play a game of Tsatsun with.

As it was, seeing Marna standing here alive, looking so much like Lindy, she struggled. It was difficult to see someone who reminded her so much of her friend, difficult for her to think about what she had lost. And she owed it to Lindy to get past that. Lindy would've wanted her to. Lindy would've wanted her to make sure that she kept others safe, make sure others didn't have to suffer the same way she had.

"Why have you drawn me out here?" Marna asked.

"Some questions."

Marna arched a brow. "Questions? That's all?"

Carth shrugged. She kept an eye on the two men lying on the ground. They remained motionless. Carth hoped they stayed that way, but was prepared to hit them with another dose of the coxberry. If it came to it, she had a few more syringes loaded. They were quality syringes, mostly designed for the hospital, but Carth could use them as a delivery system for the toxins. Alex had almost seemed like she expected that of Carth.

"Now you have me. What do you intend to get from me?"

Carth kept her face neutral. "As I said, what I want is answers. Who hired the assassin?"

Marna shook her head. "I'm afraid you'll be disappointed. I don't know the answer to who hired him. As you can imagine, in my line of work, we make more than a few enemies."

"You were expecting the attack."

Marna shrugged. "Expecting, anticipating, preparing. In my line of work, I must do all of those things. If I didn't, another would replace me."

"Your appearance. This was intentional."

A smile spread across Marna's face, and it was almost enough to make Carth want to lash out, to send one of her knives flickering through the air. Marna seemed to anticipate that, and her muscles tensed. Carth suspected the woman would be able to move quickly enough that the knife wouldn't do any good. Neither would any of her syringes. She could use her shadow magic or her flame magic upon the woman, but all that would do was incapacitate her. Carth wanted answers, and for that she needed her to cooperate.

"This appearance. You don't like it? From what I hear, you're actually quite fond of this appearance."

Now Carth took a step forward unintentionally.

Marna used that opportunity to pivot, and she spun, one foot flying forward, her fist moving with it.

Carth readied for it.

She sent a deflection using the shadows, creating something almost physical with them.

Marna's attack bounced off the shadows, and Carth stood across from her. The other woman jumped, leaping higher than she should have been able to, once more kicking while flipping in the air. Carth dropped, her A'ras training taking over, sending her to the ground so that she rolled to the side.

"You're talented," Marna said. "I'm afraid that being talented isn't enough. I'm afraid that there are a great many others who have been talented as well who thought to challenge me in Asador."

"I never intended to challenge you. I wanted to gather information. Seems that you're the one who wants to challenge me."

Marna shrugged again. "I'm only willing to do what is necessary to make sure that I keep my people safe."

"Your people? You don't think that I have the same right?" As she said it, Carth sent a surge of both flame and shadow. The mixture often had interesting effects; this time she sent it in a sweeping explosion away from her, pressing Marna back. The woman blinked, giving Carth a moment to jump, drive her elbow into her back, sending Marna sprawling forward.

Carth danced back, rather than finishing her. "As I said, all I want is answers."

Marna shook her head as she pushed off the deck of the ship. Her eyes glazed for a moment before clearing, her jaw working.

She was chewing something. Whatever it was, it was the reason Marna had the powers she did. That was something she could use, if she could gain that knowledge.

Marna sat on the deck, cupping her hands across her lap. "You won't get what you want out of me. I don't have the answers you seek."

"That's where you're wrong."

Marna laughed. "You can attack me, but others will attempt to replace me. I managed to keep the network together, something none of my predecessors have ever managed. Do you think you can do better?"

Carth leaned against the railing, feeling a hint of the spray washing over her. The ship had slowed during their fight, Carth no longer using the shadows to drive it forward. It had served its purpose; she had gone as far out as she needed to. Now she was deep enough into the sea that Marna wouldn't be able to jump in and swim back. Carth didn't have an easily accessible dinghy on board either for her to steal. Given that Carth suspected she had no significant abilities other than whatever she was given through the augmentations, she didn't fear her reaching the shore easily from here.

"I don't want your network," Carth said.

Marna frowned at that. "Then why attack me? Why come after my suppliers?"

"Because your suppliers gave me access to you. You're concerned about your smuggling connections, and I'm concerned about my informational network. It is possible that we could work together."

Marna stood, shaking herself. "I've tried working with others before. It doesn't always work so well."

"For them or for you?"

"Yes."

Carth actually laughed. In spite of herself, she found herself respecting Marna. She was talented, and she was strong, something few enough people Carth had met were. If they could find a way to work together, Carth could solidify her connections in Asador, and she could begin working on the connections elsewhere.

"I need to know who supplies you with your compounds. I need to know who your herbalist is."

Marna laughed darkly. "I'm surprised that matters to you. Seeing how you don't have any use for these abilities, since you have those of your own. In Asador, we have to find other ways. There are more than a few who have abilities of their own, and we've been forced to adapt."

"Such as the Hjan?"

Marna's eyes widened slightly. "Such as them. There are others. If we don't have a strong enough front, they will be successful."

"But you have someone who supplies you. I've met others like that. There's one in particular, a woman by the name of Hoga"—Carth watched Marna's face as she said Hoga's name—"who have various concoctions that give them abilities. They use theirs to fight the Hjan. I have fought the Hjan. I have faced them more than once and prevailed. I don't need the mixtures to do so, but I do need to know where Hoga has gone to find out who sent the assassin."

"And then? What do you plan if you find out who sent this assassin?"

"What I told you from the first moment I met you. I intend to claim my revenge."

CHAPTER 18

CARTH WAITED AT THE TABLE INSIDE THE SMALL ROOM. Marna had instructed her to meet here, and Carth had agreed to it, thinking that if she didn't, she wouldn't be able to meet with Hoga. More than anything, she needed to find this woman. Alex had significant knowledge of herbs, and medicines, but she was still limited in her overall knowledge. What Carth needed was answers to who had sent the assassin to the city, so that she could not only find them, but prevent them from harming anyone else she cared about. She intended to end this assassin.

She sat alone, a lantern on the table, and said nothing while she waited.

Alex was with her, accompanying her mostly to verify what Hoga said, if the woman bothered showing herself. Carth had released Marna under the condition that she bring Hoga to her, and she suspected the woman would comply, especially after the way Carth had managed to capture her. Carth had made it clear that she would continue to attack the smugglers, and would destroy the smuggling ring completely if Marna didn't cooperate. Carth wasn't entirely certain that she wouldn't still betray her, but had taken the chance that she wouldn't.

Wind whistled outside. A storm raged, sending rain rattling against the windows. It was the kind of storm rarely seen in Asador, but the kind she had known frequently while in Nyaesh. Violent storms there were a bit more common. Carth didn't fear the rain or the wind, but she did dislike the way they prevented her from using her shadow ability to its fullest extent.

The door rattled and she stared at it, but it didn't open.

Carth slammed her hands down on the table.

Alex looked over and arched her brow.

"I'm just getting tired of waiting. I'm not sure she's even going to show," Carth said.

"You didn't give her much choice but to respond."

"She had a choice, but I think she might prefer to avoid what I've asked of her."

Another gust of wind shook the door. This time, the door opened, and two cloaked men entered, followed by Marna.

Carth watched, wondering if anyone else would follow.

"Where is—" Carth began.

Hoga followed Marna into the room. She had a heavy brown cloak with rain sheeting from it. When she peeled back the hood, her face appeared gaunter than it had the last time Carth had seen her. Her eyes still had a sharp intensity to them. She kept her graying hair pulled back into a tight bun, which gave her features an even more severe appearance.

She stopped suddenly and started to turn.

Marna grabbed her by the arm and forced her back into the room.

"After all I've done for you, this is how you betray me?" Hoga asked Marna. The rage in her voice made it nearly crackle.

"Betray? I think you have it wrong," Marna said. "I brought you here to ensure peace."

Hoga grunted. "Peace? With this one, there is no peace."

"You were the one to initiate the attack on me," Carth said. "If anyone has a right to be upset here, it would be me. You are still alive only because I was willing to let you live. After what you did, the way you used those women—"

Marna released Hoga's arm and stepped back. "Women?"

Carth glanced from Hoga to Marna, understanding

working through her. Hoga glared at Carth, and Carth decided to play this to her advantage. "Something we can discuss later," Carth said. "For now, I'd like to focus on a different issue."

"Why have you brought me here?" Hoga asked Marna. She seemed to make a point of ignoring Carth, and Carth resisted the urge to grin. She didn't blame Hoga for the sentiment; she felt much the same way towards the other woman, especially given the way she had betrayed Carth and the people of the city. But she needed Hoga, especially if she could find the source of the assassin.

Alex surprised Carth by standing. "Hoga," she began. "I need your help."

Hoga turned to her, the icy glare in her eyes not melting as she turned her anger on Alex. "You? You've betrayed me nearly as much as anyone else."

Alex stalked towards her and jabbed her in the chest with a finger. "I betrayed you? All the things that you did to those who trusted you in the city? You still walk around thinking that you're the one who's hurt by what you've done?"

Hoga grabbed the finger jabbing her in the chest and started to twist it. "I think you're ignoring your role in things," Hoga said. "If I recall correctly, you were more than happy to learn what I had to share. I didn't hear you objecting—"

Alex slapped Hoga across the cheek.

The older woman staggered back a step. Her eyes were wide.

"Objecting? I had no idea what you were doing, the way you were using what we were doing, what you were teaching me. I had no idea. Had I known, I wouldn't have agreed to participate."

Marna stepped between them. She gave Carth a hard stare, one that left the question lingering. Carth debated whether she would need to answer or if she could ignore the question. Carth decided that having Marna and her support was more important than keeping Hoga's secret.

"It seems she hasn't shared with you why she disappeared," Carth said.

"What happened?" Marna asked.

When Hoga didn't answer, Carth stepped around the table. "Only that Hoga was involved in a slaving operation based out of Asador. If Hoga had had her way, she would have seen hundreds of women smuggled south, turned into prostitutes or worse."

Marna rounded on Hoga. "Is that true?"

Hoga stared straight ahead defiantly. "I did what was necessary to protect those I cared about."

"Those you cared about?" Marna asked. "What about those other people care about? What about those who weren't able to protect themselves?"

The anger in Marna's voice told Carth that there

was something more Marna hadn't shared, something that had hardened her.

Marna had lost somebody.

Could Hoga have been responsible for that as well?

Almost too late, Carth realized that Marna was reaching for her sword.

Carth flowed forward, pulling on shadows, and grabbed Marna's arm before she could unsheathe. "We need her expertise. That's why I had you bring her to me."

"You said she was selling women."

"Was. She is no longer."

Marna stared for a moment before shaking herself. "Yes. We will use what she knows. But then she will answer for what she's done."

Hoga laughed softly. "You're both too weak to do what you should have done. Had it been up to me, I would have—"

Alex slapped her across the face again, silencing her. "We don't care what you would have done. We know what you have done."

Hoga touched her cheek and laughed darkly again. "Such judgment from one who should not be so quick to pass that judgment. You who have done far more than you want to acknowledge. Perhaps you think you can keep that from your new master, but I know what you did."

Carth glanced at Alex, whose face had blanched.

What had she missed? There was something there that she didn't understand, but she needed to ask later. For now, what she needed was to discover what Hoga knew.

Carth slipped a knife out of her pocket, surging on the flame as she did. Hoga glanced over to her, almost as if knowing.

Could Hoga detect her using her powers? She hadn't thought the woman had that capability, but perhaps it was something she'd ingested, some power that she given herself through a combination of medicines. If that were the case, it would make her more powerful.

Hoga took the knife and stared at the blade. "What is this?"

"That's why you're here. I need to know what that is."

"This is a knife," Hoga said.

"I know it's a knife. What I want to know is where it's from."

Hoga turned the knife over, studying the blade. The slight tension in the corner of her eyes told Carth that the woman likely recognized it.

"I don't know what it is." Hoga handed the knife back to Carth.

Carth took it in her bare hand. "But you recognized that the blade is poisoned."

Hoga's eyes narrowed slightly. "What?"

Carth nodded to where Hoga had pulled the sleeve over her hand before taking the knife. "You knew the knife was poisoned. Before you took it from me, you knew."

Hoga's eyes narrowed. "If it's poison, how is it that you—"

"Poison doesn't affect me the same as it does others," Carth said. "Now, tell me where this knife is from. I need to know who is responsible for sending an assassin into the city."

"Assassin? Is that what you think?"

"I followed the man responsible. I know what I saw."

"If you followed the person responsible for this knife, you would be dead. Even you, the great Carthenne Rel, can't withstand one of the—"

She cut herself off and sneered at Carth.

"What? What aren't you sharing?" Marna asked.

Hoga shot Marna a hard glare. "It doesn't matter. Whatever she thinks she knew was wrong. Someone else might have had this knife, but they were not who she thought they were."

"You're scared of them," Carth said. "That's why you won't share anything with us."

Hoga met Carth's gaze. "If you were as smart as you think you are, you'd be scared of them as well. The problem is, you don't know what you don't know."

"Then help me find out what I need to know. Help

me make sure others aren't attacked in the city this way."

"I find it interesting that you don't recognize it, especially considering you had the help of one of them when you destroyed my shop."

Carth frowned, and it took a moment to realize what Hoga implied. "Timothy? That's what you mean? Neeland has sellswords, but that is all they are. They're mercenaries for hire. They aren't assassins."

Hoga shrugged. "Think what you like," she said. "But I recognize the blade, and there aren't many places that would use trellis flower on a blade. A violent way to die, I think."

Carth looked at Hoga, hoping for something more, but the woman didn't say anything else.

Marna nodded to the two soldiers that had remained silent during the exchange, and they both grabbed Hoga and led her back out the door and into the storm. As Marna started to follow, Carth grabbed the woman's arm.

"You lost somebody."

Marna's face remained neutral, but her posture stiffened, enough that it became clear that Carth was right.

"You think she's responsible now?" Carth asked.

Marna sighed. "I don't know if she's responsible, but if she is, then she needs to pay for what she did." Marna started to pull free of Carth's grip before pausing and turning back to face her. "How certain are you that she was the one responsible for sending women out of the city?"

"As certain as I could be."

"How?"

"Because she tried to do the same to me. I got free. I went back, I helped free the others."

Marna stiffened even more, becoming practically as still as stone. "You... rescued others?"

Carth nodded. "Who was she?"

Marna let out a slow breath. "My sister. She was taken, like so many others from Asador have been taken. She was lost, and I've thought her dead. Hoga made it seem like you..." She shook her head. "It no longer matters."

"I didn't harm those women," Carth said.

"I believe that now."

"She might still be alive, though I can't be certain," Carth said. "I'm sorry, but it's true. I wasn't able to save everyone."

Her shoulders relaxed, as if the fight had gone out of her.

"When was she taken?" Carth asked.

"A year ago. Perhaps a little bit more."

"Did she know what you did?"

Marna shook her head. "My sister was a seamstress, wanting nothing more than to own her own shop. She was quite skilled. She was never involved in anything else."

The timing was close enough that Carth wondered if it was possible. Could she have saved Marna's sister?

"Where are those you saved?" Marna asked.

"Most who wanted to return to the city did. I offered them safety, and I've done my best to keep them as well protected as I can. Up until recently, I had been successful."

"You said most returned to the city."

Carth nodded. "Most did return to the city."

"What of the rest? What happened with them?"

"They went to a city along the coast. It's a place where I've offered them ongoing protection. Some have chosen to stay there, some have chosen to move on."

Marna took a deep breath. "You'll go to Neeland?"

Carth hadn't had a chance to think about it, but suspected that she would. She needed to know whether Hoga was right, and whether the sellswords might have been responsible for what had happened in Asador. Could they have sent an assassin to do this? She needed to find Timothy, and he had given her a way to reach him, but she hadn't expected to need to use it. Certainly, not so soon.

But what other choice did she have? She intended to see to it that she had the answer she needed. If it required her going to Neeland, she would do so. Especially if she had no other way of ensuring the sell-swords didn't make another trip into Asador. She needed to somehow ensure that they didn't think to take another job, if in fact they had taken this one.

"I ask, only because if you do go, I would go with you."

Carth had considered many possibilities, but none of them involved Marna being willing to come with her. Having her along would be valuable. With her skill, her ability to fight with whatever enhancements she had, she would make a powerful ally. But... what proof did Carth have that she wouldn't betray her? How would she know that she could be safe from Marna? A journey to Neeland would take at least a week, possibly more. She would have to study maps to determine how far it was from here, and would need to leave her network alone in the city for that entire time. She didn't worry quite as much about that, but she didn't want Marna to know that she was gone.

"I will ensure no one harms your people while we're gone," Marna said, almost as if reading Carth's mind. "But I would ask that we visit this village where you left the women before we make the trip to Neeland. I need to know if my sister is there."

Carth glanced at Alex. Without Lindy, she needed someone she could trust in the city, and though Alex had shown no interest in taking a greater role, she had proven that she had the necessary strength with the way she confronted Hoga.

"It's fine," Alex said. "You need to do this. Whatever you need of me, I'll do it."

She couldn't help but fear that it would lead to Alex's death as well.

Carth turned her attention back to Marna. "I will accept your help."

CHAPTER 19

THE SHIP ROCKED BENEATH CARTH'S FEET, SENDING HER from side to side. Carth had long ago learned to roll with the waves, no longer feeling them the same way she once had. Now, she barely slipped on the deck, keeping her grip on the wheel.

Marna stood at the railing, leaning over it, occasionally vomiting. When Carth had forced her out onto the sea, using the shadows to press the ship away from the shore, she hadn't recognized how hard a time Marna had while sailing. Then, she'd only gone at a slower pace, not even enough to get far out on the sea. This time, she was sailing north along the shore, making her way towards Praxis.

"It's easier if you stay closer to the center of the ship," Carth said.

Marna glanced back at her and wiped her arm

across her mouth. "Easier? How long did it take you to adjust to sailing?"

"Probably longer than it will take you. I suspect some of the compounds Hoga mixed for you are causing the side effects. You're probably feeling the effects of the waves more acutely than I ever have."

"I haven't taken anything in the last two days," Marna said. "I wasn't sure how they would affect me while sailing. Besides, I figured that having you on board, I didn't need to worry about protecting myself."

Carth started to smile. "I saw you taking a dose this morning," she told Marna.

The woman's mouth tightened. Then she turned back to the railing and continued emptying her stomach into the sea.

The seas were choppy, heavy wind blowing out of the north making the waves larger than any Carth had sailed on in some time. She used the shadows to buffer them somewhat, knowing that without that buffer, Marna would be in even worse shape. It helped speed them along as well, sending them gliding through the sea, the rapid pace driving them forward.

"How much farther until we get there?" Marna asked.

"Praxis is probably three days by land from Asador."

Marna looked up at her. "By land."

"By sea, it's no more than two."

Marna backed away from the railing, then stood

near the mast. "I won't fault you if you choose to return to Asador," Carth said.

"I told you that I would travel with you to Neeland. I'll stand by my commitment."

Carth nodded silently. She suspected that once Marna had checked out Praxis and discovered whether her sister was or wasn't in the village, she would refuse to go on with her. Carth had to admit that it did make her a little less anxious traveling to Neeland with the idea of Marna coming with her. It was worth the risk sailing here. The delay was only minor. Carth could take that time. It helped keep her from getting too angry.

Marna suddenly covered her mouth and raced back to the railing. Carth looked away as she continued vomiting, giving her that privacy.

The village of Praxis loomed on the shore. Carth anchored in the small bay, rolling the sails up and tying them tightly. The ship was difficult to sail with one person, but she discovered that it could be done. Marna had not been much help, though Carth had not really expected her to be. The woman barely managed to hang on.

"Why aren't we sailing all the way to shore?" Marna asked.

"Too shallow. We'll row the rest of the way in."

Marna weaved around the deck of the ship, making her way towards the port side of the ship. She looked over and noted the small dinghy tied towards the aft of the ship.

"You intend to row us in with that?" she asked.

"I think you're going to find sailing in with that is easier than sailing in with the *Goth Spald*. At least with this, you're in control. It's actually better when you're closer to the sea."

"I have a hard time believing that it will be better when we're close to the sea."

Carth laughed softly as she made quick work of untying the dinghy and lowering it into the water. She grabbed a pair of oars and jumped into the dinghy. She waited, holding a line. "Are you coming?"

Marna sighed and slowly made her way over the railing of the ship before climbing in. Once Marna was settled in the dinghy, Carth quickly rowed them to shore.

When they reached the shore, Marna climbed out of the dinghy and stood still on the rocky shore, taking deep breaths. Her eyes were closed, and her hands were clasped in front of her. She breathed slowly, in and out, before turning back to Carth. Color had returned to her face, and strength seem to have returned to her. Whatever she had taken seemed to have worked quickly.

"Why here?"

Carth shrugged. "It was close. It was accessible by the sea. It was a place where the women would be safe."

Marna frowned at her. "That's all you care about? You just want the people to be safe?"

Carth shrugged. "I won't stand by while others are harmed when I can do something. I've been given many gifts, I've seen others I care about hurt when they attempted to run from their abilities," Carth said, thinking back to her parents. That might have been the biggest driver for her. Her mother must have been descended from Lashasn, and with that, she should have been able to defend herself. She should have been able to call upon the flame, but she hadn't when she was confronted by the Hjan.

Had she only defended herself, would she still be alive today?

Her father had left Ih-lash, abandoning his people, only to be drawn back in. Had he attempted to continue his connection to his people, had he not run, thinking to protect Carth, would he—as one of the shadow born—have been able to help?

Carth had to believe that he could have.

And now they wouldn't know.

"You are not who I expected," Marna said.

"What did you expect? Did you think that I simply wanted power?"

"Have I told you how I took over my position?"

Marna asked. Carth shook her head as they made their way along the shore. It was rocky here, leading to a sharp cliff rising high overhead. Carth knew the trail up and into the city. It was a difficult climb. There was access to Praxis, but not easily. That protected these people for the most part.

"How did you assume control of the smugglers?"

Marna started to smile. "It's a little bit more than only the smugglers. I've not always been the one leading the smugglers. I used to work with my sister. She ran her seamstress shop, and I worked with her."

Marna smiled as her eyes took on something of a faraway look. "I never was all that good a seamstress. She tried to teach me—the great elder god knows that she tried—but I didn't have the same steady hand, or the same patience. What I did have was a mind for the business. I helped her find cheaper supplies so that she could charge the same for her work but make more money. I helped her find more and more suppliers willing to negotiate. Eventually, that put me in contact with some less-than-reputable people." Marna shrugged. "I soon realized how disorganized their organization was as well. I continued working for my sister, but on the side, I helped organize the smugglers. Now, we have a network, one where nothing moves through Asador without me knowing. Most of it moves through the way the council would like, getting taxed the way they would like, padding their pockets, and we keep the scraps. We skim off the top, taking little enough that we avoid too much detection."

Marna trailed off and looked over at Carth. "Why are you laughing?"

"Not what you said, just your choice of words."

"What? The fact there we're keeping things from the council? Enough moves through that they earn plenty of income off what they're taxing. Even that damned university makes plenty off what they're moving. I just ensure there's an appropriate market for those who can't quite afford the rates the council would set."

Carth had to smile. She couldn't even disagree with the intent. The woman wasn't taking from anyone other than those who already had money. In that way, Carth actually respected what she was doing.

"I spent some time in the north. A place called Nyaesh."

Marna nodded. "I know of Nyaesh."

"When my parents died, I lived on the streets. I was taken in by a nice couple who sought to protect me. They took in others like me, though I don't know that I ever learned quite why."

That wasn't entirely true. Vera and Hal had worked to protect the descendants of the Reshian, trying to keep them safe within Nyaesh. They thought they could keep others safe by keeping them in the city. For the most part, they were right. Carth had been safe, however briefly that had been.

"When I was there, when I was first learning to use my abilities, I would collect scraps from those with more than me."

Marna began to laugh. "You were a thief?"

"I don't know that I would've considered myself a thief, but that's what I was. I thought I was taking what I needed, that I was only doing what others would have done. Most of those people didn't miss what we took."

"And what did you do with your earnings?"

"Most of it I gave to Vera. She used it to buy our protection. I didn't know that at the time."

"Why are you here?" Marna asked.

She had stopped, not making her way up the rocky incline towards Praxis. Instead she fixed Carth with a hard gaze that studied her.

"Many reasons, but mostly the vow I made to some dangerous people."

"What vow was that?"

"One where I was determined to see that they stopped hurting those I cared about. I wanted to see that they stopped hurting others who were powerless to stop them."

"And you intend to do this yourself? You intend to see that they don't harm others?"

Carth nodded.

"How are you able to ensure these people's safety?"

Carth glanced at Marna before starting back up the slope. "Because I've shown that I'm willing to kill them, and I might be the only one who can."

Carth picked her way up the slope, not bothering to look back to see if Marna would follow. She heard the woman's heavier breathing as the incline became steeper, but Marna didn't say anything more, leaving the questioning alone. Carth wasn't sure how she would answer more questions if Marna asked them.

The woman deserved answers, and Carth was surprised to find that she was an interesting conversationalist as well. In that way, she seemed to have more in common with Lindy than just the cut of her hair and the complexion of her skin.

When they reached the top of the rock, Carth hesitated, waiting for Marna.

"You never told me what you intend in Asador," Marna said.

Carth turned back to Marna, looking past her and towards the sea. The sky was a darkened sheet of gray. Massive waves rolled in from far out on the sea, crashing against the shore. The *Goth Spald* rocked in those waves, seeming so small from her position up here. She turned her attention to Marna. "I don't intend to seek power, if that's what you fear."

"No? I think that you've already acquired power, don't you? There is power in the knowledge you're acquiring, isn't there?"

Carth could only nod. That was the kind of power she sought. She didn't want to rule in Asador, but she wanted access to knowledge, the kind of knowledge that would help her defeat the Hjan if it came to it. But she didn't want any more power than that.

"You can keep your smuggling ring and its power," Carth said. "That's not what I'm looking for. I've never wanted to take that away from you, or those you're working with, but I will make sure that you don't harm those that I care about."

Marna offered a hint of a smile. "I have no doubt that you will."

They continued towards the village. Praxis was comprised of many thatched roofs, stout river rock walls, and even a low wall that surrounded the village itself. There was a certain quaintness about it, one that she appreciated more the longer that she was in Asador.

"You might not want it, but you do have power," Marna said.

Carth glanced over at her as they approached the village. She hoped that Praxis would hold her sister, if only to have made Marna's trip worthwhile. She doubted that Marna would travel along with her to Neeland, and even if she did, she wasn't sure that she could be trusted. The only way that would change would be if her sister was in Praxis. Even then, it wasn't a given that Marna could be trusted.

Carth thought the likelihood of her sister being in the village was low. If she was a successful seamstress, it seemed that she would've returned to Asador, to those she knew, those who cared about her and worried about her. That she hadn't... that made it likely that Hoga had been responsible for another loved one's death.

"The only power I seek is that to keep those I care about safe," Carth said as she entered the village. There was nothing else for her to say.

CHAPTER 20

CARTH MADE HER WAY TO THE VILLAGE. MARNA followed her, saying nothing more than what she had said before. Carth felt a hint of anxiety about what they would find. Would Marna find her sister? Would it matter?

They were met at the gate by a pair of women, who stopped them.

Carth smiled widely. "Jessica. Robin."

They frowned a moment before realization dawned on them. Jessica stepped forward, opened her arms, and embraced Carth. "You returned!"

"You thought that I wouldn't?" Carth asked.

Robin shook her head. "We didn't know what to expect. You've been gone so long, we thought that you would've returned to us, visited with us before now.

That you haven't made us think you were going to leave us here."

Robin and Jessica led Carth and Marna into the village. Praxis was not a big village. They had skill with wool, having mastered the weaving of fabrics, using the sheep they herded outside of the village itself for their wool. There wasn't much else that was a draw for Praxis.

Robin and Jessica led Carth to the center of the village, and she waited outside a small, finely made home while Jessica went inside. When she reappeared, an older man leaning on a cane appeared with her. He eyed Carth up and down before turning to Marna. Marna stared at him defiantly, fully recovered now from sailing with Carth.

"Ms. Rel. You have returned."

"I don't believe I've had the honor of meeting you," Carth said.

The man smiled, and Carth noted that his eyes had a film over them. She wondered how much he saw. "No, I don't believe we were able to meet. Your name is well known here, as is what you have given to these people. You added to the village."

"I want to thank you for taking them in." This wasn't the reason that Carth had come to Praxis, but it felt right thanking him. This had been the first place where she had established anything. And she was appreciative of the fact that they were also helpful.

"What prompts your return?"

Carth glanced back to Marna. "A friend of mine had someone she cared very much for abducted from Asador. I wasn't sure if she might have remained in Praxis with the others. I thought it was worthwhile coming with her, to see if she might have remained."

The chief turned his rheumy eyes onto Marna, somehow managing to see when he shouldn't have been able to. His mouth spread into a slight grin. "Friend? She watches you with suspicion, Ms. Rel. I think friend might be a little generous, don't you?"

Carth laughed. "Perhaps. Or perhaps we will be friends in time. We're looking for her sister. A woman who was once a seamstress."

The chief tapped his cane on the ground and nodded to Jessica. "Jessica can bring you to our skilled artisans. Since you left, we've had much fortune."

Carth smiled. "So I've heard. It seems as if trade now favors Praxis."

The chief nodded. "Favors us, and we are finally able to keep supplies. The village thrives. We have you to thank for it, Ms. Rel."

"I'm thankful you were able to offer your protection. The women I rescued deserved safety, not suffering."

The chief seemed to watch Carth, though it was difficult to tell with the way his eyes appeared. "Perhaps I will escort you myself." He turned to Jessica. "Would you help Sarah while I do this?"

Jessica smiled warmly, and Carth had the sense that she didn't mind at all helping Sarah. She didn't recognize the name, and wondered if Sarah was someone she had rescued, or if she was a native of Praxis.

The chief guided them through the village, taking her to the north side, away from where most of the homes were situated. From here, Carth could hear a steady hammering, one that sounded almost as if it came from a blacksmith, though the hammering was softer, less intense than what she'd heard from blacksmiths. The chief made his way through the village, weaving as he went. He leaned on his cane, but didn't seem infirm or frail otherwise. Carth was taken aback by the number of shops they passed. When she'd been here before, she didn't recall this many village shops active.

She looked over to the chief for confirmation, but he didn't pause.

When they reached the wall surrounding the northern side of the village, he stopped. Here Carth noted a row of three low buildings, each apparently new construction. The stone was freshly laid, and the roofs were neatly thatched. Thick trails of smoke escaped out of the chimneys.

"We have several places that we've had to add on

to," he said to Carth. "Since you came, we found an increased need for those with different talents. Not only have we needed our skilled seamstresses and weavers as well as those who know dyes, we've had to add masons and carpenters. Praxis is growing."

Carth hadn't heard that Praxis was booming quite like this. She was pleased to see it, though. If her small influence could lead to this much of a change in the village, she hoped that there were other positive changes as well.

The chief looked from Carth to Marna, his gaze lingering on her a moment. Carth wondered again how much he could actually see through his cloudy eyes. Marna met his gaze and returned it with a certain defiance.

Carth smiled inwardly. There was something about the defiant manner with which Marna carried herself that was enough to make her laugh. The woman was interesting, and Carth began to hope that she actually would follow through on her promise to travel with her to Neeland. She would need her expertise. She might need her organization as well.

The inside of the shop was awash with bright lantern light. The air carried the scent of oil from the lanterns, mixed with the heady scent of the dyes used in the fabrics, along with that of the smoke from the hearths. Carth surveyed the room, noting nearly a dozen women working at tables. Most were sewing, their hands moving with practiced movements, while others worked with fabrics, and a pair of older women —both of whom Carth recognized—worked at a loom.

Marna gasped and raced towards one of the women.

Carth watched, noting the similarities between them. The woman was probably a few years older than Marna, but she had wide eyes that were softer, and did not have the same hardened expression Marna possessed. She threw her arms around Marna and they began talking quietly.

The chief looked over to Carth. "It seems your friend found her…"

"Sister. It would be her sister."

"They appear close. It makes you wonder why she never returned to the city."

Carth nodded. She had wondered the same, but hadn't had any answer from Marna and hadn't felt the need to press.

"We have a great number of women who have remained in Praxis. Many feared for their safety were they to return to Asador."

"I promised them that I would keep the city safe for them," Carth said.

"It's one thing to hear you make a promise; it's another to see it enacted. They have experience with what happens in the city. Most know that safety is not guaranteed. Most recognize that there are others with power in the city."

Carth grunted. "Yes. I've come to realize that as well and have had to work through several issues that have come up. Not the least of which was a woman with much knowledge who thought to turn against others. I consider it unfortunate that she has done so."

The chief nodded. "There were some initial safety concerns here as well."

Carth shot him a look. She hadn't heard that.

The chief tapped his cane on the ground. "We have worked through them. There were a few who thought that adding these women would strain our capacity. They didn't have the vision to see what could be." He turned to Carth and smiled. "I may not see quite as well as I once did, but I still recognize an opportunity for my people."

"Only your people?"

The chief swept his hand around in a wide motion. "I've claimed them as my own. That protects them, grants them whatever safety I can offer."

Carth had done something similar. It was how she had forged the alliance with the Hjan and the A'ras and the Reshian. Since then, she'd used her connections for the same. She would do anything to protect those she cared about. She sensed from the chief that he felt much the same.

"What now for you?"

Carth nodded to Marna. "It depends on what she decides. Someone I care about was taken from me."

"And you are after revenge? I thought you above such petty things, Ms. Rel."

"Not revenge, not entirely. There is information that I need. I don't know why the attacker was sent. She claims it was for her, but I'm not convinced that was the case."

The chief tapped his cane once more on the ground. "You think they came for you."

Carth nodded.

"And they are a threat to what you intend."

"Anyone who would attack indiscriminately is a threat. That's why I intend to find out who was responsible, and what must be done to avoid it happening once more."

The chief glanced from Carth to Marna. "Where do you travel?"

"Neeland."

The chief lifted his cane but did not set it back down again. "There are many risks in Neeland. I hope you recognize the dangers you place yourself in by going there."

"The man who helped me rescue these women was from Neeland."

"Not all men are like him. Most care only about the coin. They're hired mercenaries. I would advise you to be cautious, but I suspect you are always cautious."

"I appreciate your insight. I'm hopeful that Marna will accompany me."

"Her? She has no ability—" He blinked his rheumy eyes and tipped his head as he studied Marna. "I see now. She has the knowledge of the Caulad."

Carth hadn't heard that term before. "What is the Caulad?"

"There are those who study for healing, there are those who study for harming. There is a balance between them. That is the Caulad."

Carth frowned. She hadn't realized there was an organization like that. Each time she thought she was beginning to piece things together, each time she began to think that she knew the next move she needed to make, she was again reminded of how little she truly knew.

"Do you know how to find others of the Caulad?" Carth asked. If he'd heard of them, it followed that he would know how to find them.

"Once, perhaps, but not any longer. I'll listen, and if you fail in Neeland, return to me, and I will see what I can learn. There was a time when we were limited here in Praxis, but knowledge flows through here, the same way as trade does. Perhaps I can be of use to you."

Carth sighed. The only thing left for her to know

was whether Marna would return to Asador or whether she would accompany Carth north.

Marna answered that by leaving her sister and heading over to Carth, ignoring the chief entirely. "When do we leave?"

Carth glanced to the chief. "We can go now, if you're ready."

CHAPTER 21

THE SHIP ROLLED BENEATH THEM. CARTH WAS IMPRESSED that Marna seemed to be handling the journey better this time than she had the last. Her face was still a washed-out pale shade, and she vomited a few times, but nothing like on the journey from Asador to Praxis. In fact, she even managed to join Carth at the helm a few times.

From here, the journey to Neeland would be several days. Several days spent crossing the wide-open rolling sea. Several days under the gray skies. Several days where she pulled upon her shadow blessing, drawing strength as she sent them moving as quickly as she could.

Despite that, she didn't regret the need. She wanted to find answers, and now had only more questions, especially after meeting with the chief. There were things he knew, information he possessed about the Caulad that Carth would need to follow up on, but for now, she would remain focused.

"What do you usually do while sailing?" Marna asked.

They had been gone from Praxis for the better part of half a day. Despite the haze, Carth could tell the sun had reached its midday peak, but it still wasn't very warm. The wind gusted as it so often did out of the north, sending occasional larger swells slamming into the ship. Carth noted the way Marna fought against the urge to vomit, keeping her jaw clenched, holding her focus. It was almost heroic in a way.

"Most of the time, I try to simply focus on the sea," Carth said. "I haven't been sailing alone for all that long."

"No? What were you doing before that?"

Carth turned her attention to the ship. When she'd sailed with Guya, it had been easier. She hadn't had the responsibility of making certain the sails unrolled the way they were supposed to or maintaining the lines, or even sealing the deck. She had learned the keys to navigation from him, had learned how to read charts and maps and how to rig the sails.

"Just know that I haven't sailed alone for long," Carth said.

"Well, I need something to take my mind off of what we're doing." Marna gripped the mainmast with her arm, her knuckles white as she did. She stood stiffly, her jaw clenched, as she fought back the urge to unload the contents of her stomach.

Carth sighed. She didn't have much to offer. Except... there was one thing.

"Have you ever heard of the game Tsatsun?" Carth asked.

Marna narrowed her eyes. "No. What kind of game is it?"

"Hold this," she said, guiding Marna to hold the wheel. The seas were relatively calm, considering what they'd experienced in the last few days. Marna could hold the position for now. Carth could always correct for anything when she returned. She hurried below the deck and found the board with the pieces where she and Lindy had left it. She felt a surge of sadness, thinking back to her friend and missing her again. Lindy had shown promise in the game. With much more time, Carth thought she could have made her a strong player. She had discovered the key to focusing on a different perspective, recognizing how that influenced her moves. It was something Carth had struggled with at first, until boredom had made her learn.

But Marna might actually be talented at playing Tsatsun. She had skill with coordinating and organizing her faction within the city. That proved a certain determination, one that Carth recognized could be useful.

Carth carried the board and the pieces up to the deck. Marna manned the wheel, holding on to it tightly. Carth assumed command and set the board down, quickly arranging the game pieces. She wasn't certain how stable the game board would remain while sailing but had forgotten how there were small magnets underneath the board as well as on each piece that held them in place. It was a sailing board, one Carth had realized she needed when she'd found it.

Marna watched as Carth set up the game, saying nothing. Carth walked her through the various pieces, explaining how they were used. It was a little different than how she had learned from Ras, and a little different from what she had discovered from the books, but it seemed a sensible way to begin explaining how to play the game to someone who had never played before.

"The winner is the one who moves the Stone to the opponent's side of the board," Carth finished.

"I presume you're a skilled player?" Marna asked.

"I'm not untalented," she said.

"When was the last time you lost?"

Carth thought back. She beat herself frequently, but that wasn't an honest answer. "The last time I lost was when I played the person who instructed me."

"Are there particular strategies in this game?"

"There are countless strategies. This game teaches you to anticipate and outthink your opponent. If you can put yourself in the other person's place, and you can envision how they would react and move, you will be at an advantage. There aren't many people capable enough of doing that."

"And I assume that you are?" Marna asked.

Carth nodded. "It was how I learned. I taught myself to look at the game how my first instructors would have viewed it. I thought about it from how my parents would've looked at it. I thought about it from the perspectives of people for whom I only vaguely knew how they might think. And I thought about how my enemies might play."

"I think I might like this game," Marna said.

"I'll make the first move," Carth said.

Marna studied the board, not looking up as she nodded.

―――――――――

Carth was impressed. Marna had lost the first game, but had really seemed to catch on to the idea behind how to play towards the end. Carth had been impressed with how she had finished, managing to take out several of Carth's pieces before failing. Marna had immediately begun setting up the board for another match, having apparently memorized the setup from the first game she'd played.

Carth smiled to herself. Could she have found

someone who would make a worthy opponent at Tsatsun?

This time, Carth allowed Marna to lead off. She made an aggressive move, one that reminded Carth of herself. Carth countered, and Marna made another move, one that was equally aggressive as one Carth would've made.

She knew that she shouldn't be impressed. She'd known Marna was capable—she had to be, considering the way she'd consolidated her power—but the woman had quickly grasped several of the concepts of playing Tsatsun, enough that she already seemed to be mastering how to envision the way Carth would play.

"You have an interesting technique," Carth said.

Marna stared at the board, considering her next move. "I see how you would've played."

"And now you're imagining how I would do it?"

Marna nodded.

Carth shifted her play, not wanting to win the game, hoping for a bit longer. She shifted, thinking that a strategy more like how Ras played might be more effective for Marna. It would allow Marna to partici-pate a little longer, and would give her a different style of play. Carth had to intentionally separate out how she played, struggling to remove her own style, one that was a combination of all those she'd ever played with as well as all the styles she had read about, and played Marna more as Ras.

Putting herself in his mindset was still easier. She played more conservatively this way, making moves that brought her first around the edges of the board, attempting to play less aggressively. This allowed Marna to take a few of her pieces, position herself more on Carth's side of the board, and in doing so, allowed Carth to observe her play.

From it, Carth could tell that she had a calculating mind. It was surprising the way that she struck, managing to attack more confidently then Carth would have in only her second game. Could she have found someone more than capable of countering her? Could she have found someone who could beat her?

The possibility excited her. If it were possible for her to learn this quickly, it would be more of a challenge. That was exactly what she wanted—enough of a challenge for her to need to focus on the game, for her not to be able to simply see through it.

Carth let the game play out naturally, and Marna made a few skilled moves, clearly anticipating the way Carth would play. Carth allowed her to pin her in the corner of the board before she began playing with more intensity. There was a certain thrill in nearly allowing herself to get beaten.

Finally, Carth needed to end the game, if only so they could begin again. As she began making her move, Marna surprised her, countering. Carth had to stretch herself farther than she'd expected to defeat her, but in the end, the stone moved to the Marna's side of the board, ending the game.

Marna sat with her hands in her lap, a disgusted look on her face. "I thought I was going to beat you."

"Perhaps in time. I'm happy to continue playing with you."

Marna nodded. "I would like that." She stared at the board for a little longer before shaking her head. "You surprise me, Carth. I wasn't expecting to actually enjoy myself on this journey."

Carth smiled. "Me neither."

CHAPTER 22

THE *GOTH SPALD* CUT THE WAVES WITH POWER. IT WAS part of the reason Guya had prized his ship so highly. It was a powerful ship, one that was sleek and quick. It made a perfect smuggling vessel.

Carth didn't use it that way—it was a means of transportation for her—but she valued it for many of the same reasons Guya had. Traveling across the sea could be monotonous, and now that she was determined to set up a network, she needed speed, which required the right kind of ship.

Marna remained belowdeck, finally sleeping. Carth intended to let her rest.

In the distance, the island of Neeland loomed. From the maps, Carth knew it was a massive island, one that spread for miles. The capital city of Avuan would be along the coast. Timothy had told her some of what came from Neeland, giving her an idea of what to expect, but she hadn't known much more than that. She would find mercenaries, sellswords that she could hire to help her, and hopefully men who would explain the assassin sent after her.

The wind whipped the sails, bringing them closer and closer to shore. A sliver of the moon shone overhead in the dark night, and stars twinkled. Without the stars, and without the moon, Carth wouldn't have been able to steer herself quite as easily. With them, she was able to guide the ship where it needed to go, knowing the pattern of the stars and the direction that would take her.

She eased the ship into shore, going along the side of the dock. She was pleased that Avuan had a deepwater port, preferring to pull into these docks rather than anchoring and rowing into shore.

Marna joined her on the deck as she began tying up and eyed the city with curiosity.

"You don't have to go into the city. I'm looking for who hired them."

"Just you?"

"Watch the ship. If I'm right about these men, we might need to depart quickly."

"Or they might try to steal it, you mean."

Carth shrugged.

When they were fully tied up, Carth slung a rope ladder over the railing and climbed down. It was better to do it that way rather than drawing attention to herself. As much as she could simply pull upon the shadows, she didn't want to announce herself—or her abilities—by doing so. Instead, she preferred to make her way down the same way others would have.

Once on the city street, Carth paused. The buildings were all of gray stone, the kind of stone likely pulled from the sea, and the same sort of stone that built up the seawall near where she had docked the *Goth Spald*.

A muddy dirt path led along the street front. Unlike many other places where the road was cobbled, this was nothing more than hard-packed earth turned to mud from the recent rain. Carth wished she had different boots, hating that those she wore would be damaged by the mud.

She debated where to go, thinking about how best to find the sellswords, knowing only what Timothy had shared before. He had claimed that she would be able to reach him were she to have the need, that she could come to Avuan, and that she would be able to find him, but she would need a particular token that he had given her.

Carth reached into her pocket and pulled out the strangely shaped coin. She remembered well the conversation they'd had when he had given her the coin. She had asked if she needed to find him in a tavern, thinking that was the most likely place she would've found someone like him in Nyaesh or even Asador. Timothy had smiled and shaken his head.

"Neeland has a different approach to one of my skill. You need to take this to a building with a sign that matches it. Once there, you will find someone who can help you."

"Only one that matches this?"

He had nodded. "You will find other, similar shapes. They will represent differing groups of men for hire. Some will be more or less receptive to what you have to sell. I would caution you to be careful in approaching some of these others. All are well trained. But not all will show the same consideration that I have shown."

Carth remembered smiling then. When she had first met Timothy, she hadn't thought he had much consideration for her. All he had wanted was to infiltrate the slavers, searching for information on how to find Guya and his family. She hadn't known it at the time, but he had provided invaluable help.

And now she had to find him again. She wasn't certain that she would be able to, even with his coin. Traveling in the dark and unusual city, she worried that she might be forced to use her abilities, which would expose her to other mercenaries.

Carth scanned the signs on doors as she made her way along the street. She wasn't exactly sure where Timothy would be found, knowing only that she had the coin he'd given her. With that, he claimed she'd be able to find him, or at least someone who could lead her to him.

As she made her way along the street, she noted that there weren't the usual storefronts that she was accustomed to seeing in other cities. Instead, each building had a symbol much like the one on her coin.

Carth paused, looking at one of the symbols. They were intricate, made of patterns that she suspected had meaning to the people of Neeland. She held her coin up, comparing it to the door she stopped in front of. On the coin, there were three triangles, each offset. A small circle was situated within each triangle and a single dot at the middle of each circle. The triangles were placed within a rectangular shape, one with hazy edges. She suspected that was important, though didn't know why.

Her gaze went to the door. On it, she saw a pattern with similar triangles, but no circles on the inside and no dots. There was a rectangular shape around triangles.

How was she going to find Timothy this way?

If each of the shapes were so similar, Carth imagined she would have a difficult time determining a difference. It wasn't the same as seeing images or letters… though, she realized, that might be exactly what they were. This could be simply Neeland's formal writing.

In the darkness, it was difficult to make out the shapes. Now that she saw how difficult this would be, she realized she probably should come back in the daylight. Yet, at night, she enjoyed the fact that the streets were empty, and that she didn't have to fight through crowds. She didn't know how populated Neeland would be, or how dangerous it might be in the daylight, but at nighttime, with just her in the shadows, she didn't feel nearly as uncomfortable as she might during the daytime.

Carth sank into the shadows, drawing them around her, and made her way along the street. She scanned the doors as she went, keeping the image of the pattern found on the coin burned in her mind. She found many different shapes. Some were quite different, making it easy to exclude them; others were much less obvious, at least to her. There were many similarities, sometimes so many that it was hard for her to distinguish them with any real certainty.

She paused, looking along the street before turning, making her way away from the docks. She didn't travel with any sort of goal in mind, other than simply scanning each doorway as she passed, looking for a match to the coin. As she wandered, she felt increasingly certain of the futility of trying to find Timothy this way.

What had he been thinking to believe that she could find him by simply matching her coin to his doorway?

She let out a frustrated breath, resigned to return to the ship and search during the daylight. Marna could help then. The ship would be safe in the harbor at day, wouldn't it?

As she neared the main street, she saw movement. She hesitated, sinking into the shadows, but realized that the men were coming directly towards her. As they did, she noted a dull glint of steel.

With sudden certainty, she realized that not only could they see through the shadows, they were coming for her.

CHAPTER 23

CARTH PREPARED FOR A FIGHT. SHE HADN'T WANTED TO fight, but these men approached with determination. She counted three—enough that a fight would be difficult, especially knowing the skill Timothy had possessed with the sword. The fact that these men were out at night made her suspect they would be as skilled as him. Men didn't simply come out at night unless they were able to protect themselves.

She didn't want to end in violence. She hadn't come here to kill, she'd come to seek allies.

She thought about her options, but none were ideal. Still, it was better for her to run than to get into a battle she wasn't prepared to participate in.

Carth sank more deeply into the shadows.

As she did, one of the men sprinted towards her. He moved faster than she would've expected, almost as if he were powered in the same ways she was. She had seen Timothy fighting, knew that he had significant skill with a sword, but she hadn't thought him to be powered in any sort of way.

Did these men have abilities?

What had she come for? The answer was obvious. Understanding. The mercenaries. She needed to discover what had happened in Asador.

Though she might not have found Timothy, maybe she'd found others like him.

Her mind worked through the possibilities. She could run, lose track of them, possibly return to the ship, although there was a danger that they would find her there, or she could stay and see what they might know. That carried the most risk, especially if they attacked.

She didn't know whether they had a way of deflecting her abilities, the same way that Hjan could deflect the A'ras magic, or the same way Ras had shown he was able to counter both shadows and the flame. Even Hoga had proven able to counter her ability, though hers was a more natural approach, one that came from knowledge of plants.

Carth released the shadows. She stood with her hands raised, and the nearest man racing towards her stopped suddenly.

She forced herself to keep aware of the sword. Her own sword was sheathed, and though she was skilled with it, she didn't think she had the same level of skill as Timothy, so it was unlikely she had the skill of others like him. She was no mercenary.

"A Reshian," the man said.

He had a hoarse voice, and through the darkness, she noted a hooked nose, a face scarred by pox. He had eyes that disappeared into the hollows of his cheeks, and short black hair. There was a confident laziness to his posture, and she had the sense that he was coiled, as if ready to strike were the need to arise. Carth didn't want to give him any reason to do so.

"I'm not Reshian. I am descended from Ih-lash, and possess shadow skills, but I'm not Reshian."

"If you have the shadow ability, you're with the Reshian."

Carth shook her head. As she did, the man pulled back his sword, preparing to attack.

With a surge of power, she sent the energy of the flame through the palm of her hand, pressing out and toward him.

He staggered back and held his sword up in a defensive pose. At least she knew the flames worked here.

"I am not with the Reshian."

The other two Neelish men reached the other. He glanced at them and they shook their heads. The first man slammed his sword into his sheath.

"Why are you here?" he asked.

Carth considered showing them the coin. If she did,

would she be brought to Timothy? His warning rang in her mind. He had cautioned her about the people in his homeland, warning her that there was danger here, and that if she were to find any others besides him, she might be subjected to that danger.

Carth palmed the coin, preferring not to show it just yet. "I'm in search of some men."

One of the other men, a shorter one, with a more youthful face but the same hook to his nose as the lead man, started to snicker. The lead man shot him a hard look and he silenced.

"You think to hire someone?"

Carth glanced from his face to the others with him. She wasn't certain she was reading this situation right. Something didn't feel quite right for her.

"I need mercenaries. I hear they can be hired in Neeland."

The lead man grinned. "Hired, yes. But the price is high. Are you prepared to pay?"

Carth reached for her pocket, and the lead man quickly unsheathed a short sword, moving faster than she could believe was possible. She would need to be careful with them. Possibly more careful than she had realized.

"If you'll give me a chance, I will show you that I have the funds to pay for what services I need."

The man nodded.

Carth continued reaching into her pocket, drawing

out a coin purse. She had filled this one with fifty gold coins. Gold would be valuable regardless of where she'd acquired it, making the fact that it was Asador gold less of an issue. That she had Asador gold also provided her with another benefit as well. It would help prove to him that she wasn't Reshian.

She opened the purse, showing a flash of gold, noting the hungry look to their eyes as she did.

Carth slipped the purse back into her pocket. "As I said, I'm looking to hire"—she shot a look to the younger man—"a few men. I have a task I need performed."

"What sort of task?" the man asked.

Carth considered them for a moment. She made a play of taking her time, letting them think she needed that time in order to come to the decision. She already wasn't certain she could trust them.

"The job would be mostly training."

The man frowned at her. "Most don't hire Neelish swords for training purposes."

Carth shrugged slightly. It was the barest of movements of her shoulders, enough to draw attention to it, but trying to play at nonchalance. She wasn't certain she succeeded. Perhaps not usually. But… "That's the job. Do you have men for hire?"

The man's gaze drifted to her pocket before returning to her face. When it did, he nodded once. "We have men for hire, though for what you're requesting, I don't know that you'll need that many. That raises the price, you see."

"Is that right? I would imagine you charged on a per-unit basis."

Carth inwardly thanked Guya for all the times she'd worked with him, trading. Not only had she gained knowledge of sailing and the terminology of the sea, but she had gained an understanding of what was required for trading purposes. Guya had always been concerned about the unit price. He always claimed that was what was mattered. He might buy in bulk, but he sold in smaller quantities. That was where he made his money.

"You ask about the unit price of soldiers? These are men, not spools of thread or sacks of grain."

Carth glanced at the three men. Instinct told her not to trust them, and she had learned over the years to trust that instinct. There was something that wasn't quite right here, something she didn't fully understand. She wished she had found Timothy's mark, so that she could have found men like him.

And maybe that was the key. Maybe she needed to ask about their mark.

"Which house is yours?" she asked.

The men glanced at each other.

"House? What you mean by this?" the man asked.

Carth pointed to awards the nearest doorway. "The symbol. Which one do you affiliate with?"

The man shook his head. "The Neelish swords are all the same. What does it matter?"

Bells practically rang in her head. That ran counter to what Timothy had told her, and as a man who was a mercenary, and concerned about coin, she trusted that he had told her the truth. If it didn't matter to them which one she went to and which one she hired, then he wouldn't have made a point of telling her, and providing her with a coin to use.

"Your crest. Seems like everybody has their own crest. What does yours signify?"

The man stared at her, saying nothing for a long moment. Finally, he shook his head. "Do you want to hire our swords, or do you not?"

Carth studied them. The easy answer would be to say no. Timothy had been clear about the fact that there were differing factions of soldiers and Neeland, but maybe it was possible that those factions only existed citywide. Could it be that everyone within the city was a part of the same faction?

She had to admit that it could be.

"How about before we do the training, I give you a different job?" Now she would find out what she had come to learn.

"What kind of different job?"

Carth arched brow. "You are sellswords, aren't you? What kind of job do you think I would offer a hired sword?"

The lead man stared at her. "What's the job?" he repeated.

"I'll need a dozen men. And preferably your most trustworthy ones."

"You're paying for them to be trustworthy."

"Fine. That doesn't change the fact that I need a dozen men. What's the price on that?"

"Depends on what you need them for, and for how long."

Carth did the calculations.

"Let's call it two weeks. Let's say killing might be involved."

"What kind of killing?"

"You need to find the man who carried this knife."

She pulled the once-poisoned blade from her pocket and flipped it to him. He caught it and studied it, no look of recognition on his face. That was disappointing. It would have been easier for the assassin to have been a sellsword, but this could work for her as well.

"Where did you find this?" the man asked.

"An assassin. One I want you to kill. Do you think you can do that?"

The man considered her for a moment before nodding.

CHAPTER 24

As the ship sailed away from Neeland, Carth watched the city grow increasingly distant. Marna stood next to her at the railing, no longer struggling with the same nausea she'd experienced traveling here, but her face remained pale, almost ashen.

"So you hired them for what?"

"Presumably I hired them to find our assassin."

"Presumably?"

Carth shrugged. "There's another task for them if this works out."

"If? You don't believe it will?"

Carth stared at the ship sailing behind them and shook her head. "I don't believe this will end as I hope."

"Why aren't they sailing with us?" Marna asked.

Carth laughed softly. "Mostly because I don't trust them."

"You trust them enough to use them to find this assassin."

Carth shrugged. "Finding an assassin and keeping people I care for safe are two entirely different things. One involves finding someone who has already harmed someone I care about, and another involves keeping the remainder of the people I care about safe."

"The more I learn of you, Carth, the more I realize how little I know you. Perhaps studying you a little longer will help me beat you at Tsatsun."

Carth smiled. "You can only learn so much watching someone. You need to place yourselves in their mindset in order to discover the key to their thought process. Only then can you know how to beat them at Tsatsun."

"Why do I have the feeling that even then I won't know how?"

Carth watched the narrow-bodied Neelish vessel as it split the water, keeping far enough away that she could change course if needed. The vessel held the dozen Neelish soldiers, mercenaries, men she'd hired to find this assassin for her. They believed they could, and Carth suspected they knew something, but did they know enough? Did they really know who had attacked Lindy, who had come after Marna?

Carth wasn't certain how accurate their information was, but it was more than what she'd had. And she believed they had connections she didn't. She also believed they were dangerous in ways she didn't fully understand.

Marna disappeared belowdeck for a moment before reappearing. When she did, she carried with her the Tsatsun board and game pieces. She began setting them up, moving them into place with a practiced hand. Carth could only smile and nod when Marna indicated she was ready to begin.

The Neelish ship had stopped three times at port. Each time they had gone to contacts they claimed to have, contacts Carth had not been allowed to accompany them to see. Each time, she thought perhaps she had gotten close enough to the man who had killed Lindy, only to find out that she had not. This time, the ship sailed past Asador, making its way along the coast. Carth felt a growing trepidation as it did, wondering why the sellswords would be heading towards Reva.

There was no reason for them to visit Reva, none other than the fact that Carth had established her network there and that Dara was there.

"I can see that something's making you nervous," Marna said.

It was early morning, the sun starting to creep above a clear horizon. The day would be bright, the sun warm and comfortable. And yet, troubled thoughts plagued her mind. She had a growing fear as they traveled, one that was not satiated by the occasional stops in port. When they had neared Asador, Carth had thought they were going to stop, but wasn't entirely surprised when they kept on towards Reva.

As they pulled into the small port, Carth pulled alongside them, tying up. The captain, Delpar, one of the sellswords Carth had spent time with, stepped off the ship first.

Carth met him, hand hovering near her knife. She didn't want to make too aggressive a movement, but she needed to know what was going on here. Why were these men in Reva?

"You can stay on your ship, we'll let you know if we discover anything here."

Carth met his gaze. "I intend to accompany you into this city," Carth said.

The captain shrugged. "It's your choice. Only that there is no need for you to. You won't be able to follow us to our contacts."

Carth offered a half smile. "And you won't be able to follow me to mine."

The captain studied her, then started laughing. "I would love to believe that you had your own sort of contacts. If you did, you wouldn't need us."

"I don't need you for your contacts. I need you for your skills in stopping the man I hired you to take care of."

The captain made his way up towards the city, followed by three of the Neelish sellswords. Carth watched them, studying them as she did.

When she returned to the deck of the *Goth Spald*, Marna approached. "What is it you worry about?"

Carth shook her head. It was hard to put a finger on what it was that troubled her, only that they had stopped in several port cities along the way from Neeland, and each time Carth had let them go alone. This time, she could at least discover what they were after. They didn't know that she had a way to reach them. They didn't need to know, either.

"Would you be comfortable remaining on the ship, keeping an eye on the rest of the sellswords?" Carth asked.

Marna glanced over at the ship before nodding. "You think you're going to follow them?"

"Not follow. I have another small network started here."

Marna started laughing before she realized that Carth was serious. "Why here?"

"I intend to have a network all along the coast. This was the next one in my progression."

"In Reva? The trade isn't that good in Reva. You'd be better off a little further down the shore in Thyr."

Carth's eyes narrowed. Marna must've seen it, because her breath caught.

"That's we you're after? You think to take on Venass?"

Carth shook her head. "I don't intend to take anyone on. I intend to ensure that those who've made promises will keep them. The best way I know how is to know more than they know."

Marna glanced over at the ship. "I will watch," she said. "What do you want me to do if they begin to move?"

"Find me. Come to the Red Lion and give them this." Carth fished in her pocket before grabbing a small coin. "They'll know what it means."

Marna held the coin out, twisting it. It was a Nyaesh coin, one that Carth had added her own signature to. It had been designed to send signals back to others in the north, ones that would indicate that they could come for her, but she could co-opt it for a different use.

Carth made her way off the ship, trying not to look back at the Neelish ship. It was difficult, and she found her gaze drawn to them. With four soldiers in the city, that left eight on board. It was enough that she knew she would need to be careful with them, enough that she worried about Marna were she attacked, even enhanced as she was with Hoga's concoctions.

Once up in the city, she thought back to the last

time she'd been here. What would happen if the assassins had come here? She hadn't considered the possibility, not thinking that there would be anything here for them, believing that they had been after Marna, but... she was forced to wonder if that were true.

What if there was another reason they had come to Reva? What if the real reason was Carth, and her network?

The thought troubled her as she made her way into the city and reached the Red Lion tavern. She hoped Dara was there and would have answers for her.

CHAPTER 25

CARTH FOUND THE INSIDE OF THE TAVERN TO BE LESS chaotic than the last time she'd been here. There was a certain energy here, one that came from the women that Dara managed. Carth was pleased with the way everything still seemed coordinated. She didn't recognize the two women working in the tavern, but she did recognize the way they maneuvered through it, seemingly unfazed by the presence of the others here. A few men sitting at tables attempted to grab at them, but the women shifted so that they avoided it. They were otherwise inconspicuous as they made their way around the tavern.

Carth took her seat at a booth, surveying the inside of the establishment. There was really nothing for her to say; this was designed for her to have an opportunity to simply observe, but she needed to find Dara, so that she didn't have to worry about what was taking place here.

"What's a lovely lady doing here alone?" a man said as he approached. He had a thick slur to his words, too much drink in him. He wore a faded gray cloak and made no effort to conceal the short sword strapped to his waist.

Carth glared at him. "I don't think you want anything to do with me."

The man slid into the booth on the other side of her. He leaned forward, his breath stinking of booze, and she noted a smile emerge from beneath the hood of his cloak. There was something about it that seemed almost familiar. "Everybody wants a little company," he said.

He waved to one of the waitresses, who made her way over. Carth tried to make eye contact, but the woman didn't seem to notice, or if she did, she had no reason to think that there was anything Carth could tell her.

"My friend and I here would like a tankard of ale," he said. He managed to make the words sound a little less slurred. The woman smiled sweetly and hurried off.

"I'm waiting for a friend," Carth said.

"And you found one," the man said.

Carth unsheathed her shadow knife and set it on the table. She started surging a hint of the shadows into it. "I think you're misunderstanding. You're not the friend I'm waiting for."

The man stared at the knife and then started laughing. It was a slightly wild sound, but it didn't carry very far into the tavern. Carth was frustrated, wishing he'd pull back his cloak. A man who tried to hide his features in a tavern made her slightly nervous, knowing that there weren't too many reasons someone would do that.

The waitress returned, carrying two tall mugs of ale. She set them down, and the man fished out a stack of coins, which she scooped up and deposited in her pocket before hurrying away. Carth caught the slight glimmer of silver from the coins. How much had the man paid her? Was he so intoxicated that he didn't realize that he'd drawn that much out of his pocket? She'd seen more foolish things while at the Wounded Lyre in Nyaesh, so she wasn't entirely surprised by that.

The man lifted his mug and took a long drink before setting it on the table. "Aren't you going to have a drink?"

Carth slid the knife forward a few inches across the table. "As I said, I came here to meet with a friend."

"And I said," the man said, pulling the hood of his cloak back, "you found one."

Carth suppressed a groan as she recognized Timothy. "Not drunk, I suspect, either."

"I find that giving off the appearance of drunkenness is a good way of being overlooked, don't you?" He watched Carth's face for a moment and then took another drink of his ale. His mouth twisted in a sour expression as he did. "Of course, you have to enjoy the taste of ale in order to truly enjoy its effects. Unfortunately, I do not."

"What are you doing here?" Carth asked.

"You came looking for me. I only thought to find out why."

Carth reached for the marker she had in her pocket, the one Timothy had given her before he had left following the attack they'd survived in Asador. "I came looking for you, but I didn't find you."

Timothy's eyes narrowed slightly. "No, you found something worse."

"Worse? I found men for hire."

Timothy chuckled. He took a drink of the ale and swept the hood of his cloak back up over his face. His eyes scanned the tavern, little more than pinpricks beneath the hood of his cloak. The shadows there seemed to dance and move, almost as if he controlled them, though Carth knew that he did not. Timothy was skilled, his training in Neeland giving him a dangerous competence, and she suspected he had enhanced abilities much like Marna had managed, but other than that, she knew he was not powered, not in any way similar to her. He had been a skilled ally, one she would not have been able to survive without.

"I warned you to find only this marker," Timothy said, tapping the coin in her hand.

"You didn't tell me that there were dozens of similar markers," Carth said.

Timothy shrugged. "Similar, but not the same. Even in my homeland, there are different factions. Some have less honor than others."

Carth started to smile. "I take it that you feel you have more honor than the others?"

Timothy leaned forward, the hint of ale still strong on his breath. He had another scent to him, one that was a mixture of earthy undertones, as if he'd been buried. It seemed strange here on the rocky shores of Reva. "There are men with honor you can hire for the task at hand."

"What do you know about the task I have?"

Timothy grunted. "Only that the fools you did manage to hire have been making enough noise along the coast that they brought attention to them. I thought you were cleverer than that."

Carth sighed. "It's not a matter of being clever. I'm searching for an assassin, one who worked through Asador, using this." She pulled the knife from her pocket and set it on the table across from them. "Is it anything you recognize?"

Timothy pulled a dark blue handkerchief from his

pocket and used it to take the knife. As he twisted it, studying the blade, his posture changed. His back straightened, and he seemed somewhat taller, if anything.

"Where did you come across this?"

"As I said, there was an assassin in Asador who thought to eliminate one of my friends."

Timothy glanced from the blade to Carth's face, noting how she held the knife. "How is it that you can withstand the effects?"

"My abilities grant me a certain immunity."

"I would imagine it's not infinite."

"How did you know?" She had nearly died on her way to find Alex, thinking that she had infinite immunity to the poison. That had been a mistake, and it was one she would not make again.

"This has a certain lifespan once it reaches the blood. I imagine that even with your strength—and I have no doubt about your strength—you would still struggle to withstand it. You can touch it, and burn it from your skin," he said, looking up into her eyes, "but I suspect that more than that is difficult, even for you."

"Whose was this?"

"Someone who has betrayed the trust of the guild."

"The guild?" Carth asked.

Timothy nodded. "There is a guild of assassins, men trained in the deadly art of using various poisons. This guild has a certain honor to it. If he eliminated one of your friends, that means he has violated the honor the guild is known for."

"How is it that you know this?" Carth asked.

"Because I am a member as well."

"I thought you were a sellsword."

"At first. The guild members are recruited from many places."

"Such as the Caulad?"

"Where did you hear that term?"

"Hoga was one of them."

Timothy leaned forward, the hood of his cloak slipping a little, and frowned. "If Hoga was a part of Caulad, then she also would have abandoned it."

Carth wondered if that was true. Hoga might have used her knowledge in ways she shouldn't have, but she hadn't been quite as dangerous as this assassin. And she still used her knowledge to benefit Marna, and others like her. In Carth's mind, that made her a little bit less like this assassin.

"Why are you here, Timothy?"

"Because you are in danger."

"Because of this assassin?"

Timothy scanned the tavern, his eyes drifting around, settling on an older couple sitting near the door before turning back to Carth. "As I was saying, some of the men from Neeland are less honorable than others. When I had given you my token, it was a way for you to find the Caulad Guild. Instead, you found sellswords."

Carth laughed softly. "Since you didn't tell me there was a difference, I didn't realize that I was searching for a difference."

"No, and you shouldn't even know about the Caulad Guild. Few who are not members do."

Carth wondered how the chief of Praxis knew. Why had he known?

"Why am I in danger from the sellswords?"

"Because—"

He didn't get a chance to finish.

The door to the tavern slammed open. Six of the sellswords slipped in, each with swords unsheathed. Two of the men sitting near the door jumped up, both unsheathing swords. Timothy closed his eyes before blinking them open.

"As I said, danger."

He jumped, flipping knives from beneath his cloak.

Carth had seen Timothy fight before, but he moved with a lithe grace, one that reminded her of Marna.

Carth grabbed the shadow knife from the table and used it as well as the flame knife as a focus, pressing her power through them as she met the sellswords. She counted six still standing. Three more men suddenly appeared in a corner, and Carth realized she'd underestimated their numbers. She wondered if the sellswords had been arranging things so that they would meet in

Reva, using this as a base to attack. How had they known Carth would come here to this tavern?

Unless… unless they had somehow already overpowered Dara.

Timothy turned to face the three men in the corner, leaving Carth with the six. Normally, the odds would be in her favor, but these mercenaries fought with a fluid grace, one that Carth struggled to defend against. In addition to that, she had only her knives, and they had swords.

She needed to balance the scales.

Carth pulled upon the shadows, using them to strengthen her, and flipped over to the nearest man, jabbing her knife into his back and twisting. As he dropped his sword, she grabbed it and spun. Now armed with both sword and knife, she faced five remaining sellswords. The odds still weren't good.

The door slammed open once more, and Marna darted in. She was a blur of power, cutting down two of the sellswords before they realized there was another opponent. One of the sellswords turned to face Marna, leaving Carth with two. Carth smiled darkly.

Pulling on the shadows, she shrouded herself in them and darted forward, slicing at the two men. They managed to block.

A burst of color appeared in the air, the same as what Hoga had used against her.

Carth swore to herself. Bursting through her flame

magic, she burned away the effects of the power. She would have to find a different way to fight.

Pulling on the shadows, she jumped again, kicking as she did. One of the men managed to grab her leg, but she swung with her other, crashing into his head. She fell to her side, kicking again with her good leg. Breath burst out of her. The remaining sellsword stood over her, his sword slicing down towards her.

And was stopped.

In one fluid motion, he was beheaded.

Carth looked up and saw Dara standing over her, holding one of the sellsword's blades. She shook her head.

"Carth, it's good to see you, but maybe next time you won't destroy the tavern?"

Carth could do nothing other than laugh.

CHAPTER 26

THE INSIDE OF THE TAVERN HAD BEEN CLEANED OF THE bodies of the fallen mercenaries. Between Dara and the other women working with her, she managed to get them moved quickly, cleaned out of the way so that they didn't have to stare at the dead. Carth sat in a corner booth, eyes scanning the tavern as she sat. Timothy sat across from her, no longer making a show of hiding himself within his cloak.

The other servers in the tavern appeared shaken. They might have done some training, and had gained some expertise with using different combination of concoctions, but that wasn't the same as actually facing another opponent, certainly not someone quite as skilled as these sellswords were.

Dara came in through the kitchen door and quickly surveyed everything before coming to join Carth at the table. She wore a short sword at her waist that seemed fitting given the leather pants and comfortable jacket she had on as well. This was not the same Dara Carth had met back when she'd first departed with Guya. This was a confident woman, one who was in charge of her surroundings.

In that respect, Carth thought that Dara being on her own, and having Dara not require Carth, was beneficial. That had given the woman a chance to gain a certain independence, as well as a confidence. Would she have managed to gain either of those had she remained with Carth?

"Well. That was a royal shitstorm."

Timothy arched a brow. "How long have you been in Reva?"

"A few months. Why?"

Timothy shrugged. "Only that that is the kind of comment I would've expected from someone who's been in Reva their entire life."

Carth laughed. "Dara has always been advanced when it comes to her swearing."

A slight flush worked across Dara's face before fading. "Sometimes I think about what my family would think of me now. I'm quite a bit different than the girl who was abducted from her home."

Timothy met her gaze. "You either change, or you die. This world is not meant for those unwilling to face it head-on. But, for those who are able and willing to see the world a different way, who are willing to face it, and test themselves, they can grow, and become powerful."

"Like Carth?" Dara asked.

Timothy looked to Carth and fixed her with a hard gaze. "There aren't too many who are quite like Carth. Sometimes I think that's not necessarily a bad thing."

Dara forced a tight smile before turning her gaze to Carth. "What happened here? When I realized there were mercenaries in the tavern, I had the others clear out. Then I realized you were here too."

"How long did you know there were mercenaries here?" Carth asked.

Dara's gaze darted around the tavern. "There have been men arriving for the last week or so. Mostly they've been found around the town, but a few made their way into the Lion, and when they did, I was able to observe what they were after. I'm still not certain what brought them here."

Carth shook her head. She wasn't certain either. She turned her attention to where Marna sat at a table in the middle of the tavern. Carth had asked her to remain there while she determined what she needed to do. Marna had taken only a slight offense to it, but Carth didn't want to involve her in the work Dara did until she knew a little bit more. Marna could be useful, but there remained a part of Carth that still didn't completely trust the woman. She wanted to—especially after spending days sailing with her, gaming with her, and learning more about what had driven her—but Carth had been misled before and had learned to be careful. With Guya managing to manipulate her the way he had, Carth knew she needed to be careful.

"I thought I knew why they were here," Carth said. She sighed softly. "I'm no longer certain."

"Well, they came to the Lion. Do you think they intended to disrupt the network forming here?"

Timothy answered this time. "Those men don't care about who they were here for. All they cared about was the coin."

"I'm the one who hired them. I'm the one who had the coin." Carth couldn't believe that those she'd hired had been responsible for attacking. Had it not been for Timothy appearing, and even for the presence of Dara and Marna, they might've been successful.

"You might've hired them, but it's possible there was another buyer, one with deeper pockets."

"What's this about?" Dara asked. "Why have you returned to Reva?"

Carth sighed once more. She hated that she had to tell Dara about Lindy's passing, but the two of them had never been all that close. What Carth hated more was that she was forced to think about it, that she had to recall what had happened to her friend. All she wanted was to move past it, but would she ever be able to?

Losing Lindy hurt in ways that losing her mother and father never had. It was more personal; it was someone who was close to her, and who she should have been able to protect, but had not managed to do so. With her mother, Carth had been ignorant of her own abilities, and her mother—if she had powers of her own—should have been able to keep herself safe. Even her father should've managed to help. He had abilities with the shadows and was shadow born himself. No, losing her mother had been difficult, but it hadn't pained Carth the way losing Lindy had.

"Lindy was killed," Carth said.

Dara's eyes widened slightly. "What? How?"

Carth licked her lips, swallowing against the pain she felt there. "She was taken out by an assassin. There was a man moving through Asador, and we tried to stop him…"

Dara reached across and grabbed Carth's hands. "Oh, Carth, I'm so sorry."

Carth nodded. What else was there to say?

"And that's why you're here? You're after revenge?"

"Perhaps at first. That was what I wanted, but now —now I worry there is more at play. I thought they were after Lindy, partly because she looks like Marna."

"That's who's with you?" Dara's gaze shifted to Marna, sitting at a table by herself.

She had a mug of ale sitting in front of her, one that one of the servers in the tavern had managed to acquire for her. She sipped at it quietly, her eyes drifting around the tavern, never resting. There was a quiet confidence to her, one that didn't fear the fact that she was in an unknown environment, didn't fear the fact that she sat by herself, outnumbered by others were an attack to come to her. Carth noted that her hand occasionally went to a pocket of her cloak. Was that where she stored Hoga's concoctions? What would happen if Carth were to try one of those concoctions? Would she gain even greater abilities?

There wasn't much purpose for her to add additional enhancements to her shadow ability or to the Lashasn heritage. Doing so might make her stronger, but it wouldn't necessarily give her any other benefit.

"Marna leads the smuggling guild within Asador," Carth said. "I thought they were after her..."

"Why would anyone care who leads the smuggling guild?" Dara asked.

"There are many who would care who runs the guild," Timothy said. "The guild is responsible for maintaining a supply of various items within the city. They allow those without access to the university, or others like them, to acquire the same type of goods."

"The university would know they exist," Carth said. "They may not care for it. But there's very little they can do to prevent it completely." Her mind started working through what had bothered her since learning of the guild, and learning about the underground tavern, and learning even of Marna.

There were few who knew what Marna looked like. That much Carth had been certain of. Marna had managed to stay in the shadows almost as much as Carth did. Doing so meant that few would have recognized her, and fewer would have recognized that Lindy looked like her. It was possible that Marna had dressed herself so that she would appear more like Lindy, so that she could remove a threat from the city, but that made little sense to her.

Carth got up suddenly and went over to Marna's table.

She sat in front of her, hands flat on the table, a hard gaze fixed on the woman.

"What did Hoga do?" she asked.

Marna glanced briefly over to where Timothy sat with Dara before turning her gaze back to Carth, shaking her head. "Hoga didn't have anything to do with what happened to your friend."

Carth's mind started working through things, piecing together what she knew. Marna hadn't known about Hoga's role in her sister's disappearance, and when she had discovered it, she had suddenly become willing to help Carth. What was the connection?

"It wasn't Hoga, was it?"

Carth started playing out the game that had formed in her mind. Marna was smart, skilled, and a natural

Tsatsun player. She was a planner, one who had assumed control of the smuggling guild, something Carth suspected was not an easy task. For her to take that place, it meant that she likely had coordinated many different moves in order to assume that control.

Carth swore under her breath. She should've seen it before.

"You wanted my network out of the way. You thought us a threat. You arranged for the assassin."

Marna started to shake her head before she stopped herself. "I wanted to send a message. Hoga claimed a contact. It went... wrong."

"Wrong?"

"I didn't intend her to bring an assassin to my city. I wanted to disrupt what you were doing, slow you. That's all." She took a deep breath. "I did only what was necessary to protect those I'm responsible for."

It felt like betrayal, much like when Guya had betrayed her, only this one... this one was different in some ways. Carth almost understood the reasoning, but not why she had concealed it from her. "Why not tell me? Why hide from me your role in what happened in Asador?"

"After what we've seen, what I've shared with you, you still feel the need to ask?"

"I'm not sure what I need to ask about."

"I didn't know she was responsible for my sister's disappearance. I didn't know. I thought..."

"You thought it was me?"

Marna nodded.

"Had you known, what would you have done differently? Would you have attempted to have Lindy assassinated anyway? She was still a threat to your rule, especially if you feared her trying to wrest control of the smugglers from you."

"You of all people should understand how I have done what was necessary to protect those I'm charged with keeping safe."

Carth's mind still raced, trying to work through everything. "When you learned of your sister, when you saw that she lived, you didn't feel it was necessary to return to Asador at that time?"

"There was a penance I needed to pay."

Carth bit back the first response, the question about the penance Lindy had ended up paying, knowing it would do no good. Snapping at Marna wouldn't change the loss of her friend. Lindy was gone.

And Carth realized that what she said now would determine whether she lost another friend. Marna could not replace Lindy, she could not restore the person who was missing, but she had begun to become a friend. Carth had few enough true friends. There were those she served, those she had vowed to keep safe, but friends? There weren't nearly enough friends.

"You helped me here. Do you feel that you served your penance now?"

Marna shook her head. "I've done nothing more than continue to attempt to erase what mistakes I've made. I will fight with you, Carth, if you let me."

Carth glanced back to Dara, and to where Timothy sat, watching her with an intense stare. Carth could choose to abandon the help that Marna offered, and she could choose to let her return to Asador, resume control of the guild—something that Marna would likely do regardless. Or she could use her help, use the strength the woman obviously possessed and borrow from it, to help her find the assassin, and get a measure of revenge.

"I will accept your help. From now on, we will keep no more secrets."

Marna nodded. She stuck her hand out, waiting for Carth to shake it. When Carth did, she felt a weight lifted off her.

CHAPTER 27

REVA WAS NOT A LARGE CITY, BUT IT WAS A COMPLICATED one, one where women like Carth could come, could work with locals, and could establish a network such as she had. It was not just the Red Lion that had joined Carth's network. Other taverns had as well, places where Carth had made a point of connecting the locals, working with them, training them.

Now they were more competent than they had been before, confident in ways they had not been. Carth was impressed at the rapid spread of Dara's network, impressed by the way Dara had coordinated it, organizing them into something that was truly unified. Information discovered in one tavern was shared with women from another, so that they all began to listen, learning from each other.

Word was out, with each knowing they sought an

assassin. They had made a point of sharing with others that Carth was in the city, something Carth had said needed to be shared so that they could draw out the assassin. More than that, they had made it clear Carth was here. It was all the better to draw out the assassin.

Darkness hung over the city, and Carth moved through it, using it to her advantage as she had so often before. Marna talked with her, drawing strength from the specific concoction that Timothy had created for her, one that was much like what Hoga used to create for her, and she padded soundlessly, easily keeping up with Carth.

As they moved between the buildings, watching for other signs of movement, Marna glanced over. "Why are we staying in Reva?" Marna asked.

"Because I intend to finish this. This assassin you hired is responsible for too much harm."

"But there are others here who will be harmed," Marna said. "Why not bring him away from the city?"

"Here I have the advantage that the others all will report to me. In Asador, there are multiple networks in play."

"But I would be able to obtain information there."

Carth nodded. "You would. But it's more than obtaining the information, it's coordinating it. It's discovering what else the university might know. It's also discovering what other networks might exist. I've only been in Asador for a short while, but I recognize that there are multiple points of access, multiple places where I need to pay attention to what's taking place. I fear that if we return to Asador, we run the risk of either the assassin not following me, or others getting harmed. At least here in Reva, there's enough of a connection with these women that I don't have to worry about others getting injured."

"Other than those within your network."

Carth nodded. "They know the risk, and take it willingly."

"Didn't your Lindy take the risk knowingly as well?"

"She did. She made the choice to follow me out into the city, knowing what we might encounter, knowing that there might be those within the city who could harm us."

She'd made the choice, and she'd made it knowingly, but Carth wondered if Lindy had really known. Had she ever truly understood what she was getting into? She had been confident in her skills, and perhaps that had come from Carth. But perhaps that had been warranted as well. Lindy had been capable. She had managed to coordinate Carth's efforts within Asador.

"But that's not the reason the real reason you've chosen to come here," Marna said.

Carth fixed on a space between buildings in front of her. The shadows seemed to slide over themselves. She was certain there was movement here, though why? What did she see?

Carth shook her head. "That's not the real reason," she agreed.

"What is it, then?"

"The real reason is that the assassin has been making his way east." Carth crept forward and glanced over to Marna. "Hoga set you up with someone to help eliminate the threat in the city," Carth said.

Marna nodded. "She did. What's your point?"

There was the thing that had troubled her. "The assassin came after Lindy because she presumably looked something like you."

Marna eyes widened, making the connection that Carth had made when she'd realized what Hoga had done. She had targeted Marna, wanting to be free of her, but had failed.

"Then why has he come to Reva? The only reason to come to Reva is because they discovered what I was doing, or my connection."

"Then why are we—"

She didn't get a chance to finish. The shadows shifted and Carth cloaked herself quickly, grabbing Marna and dropping to the ground. A knife whistled over her head as she did.

Marna gasped, and Carth clasped her hand over the woman's mouth, silencing her. She remained cloaked in the shadows, creeping slowly forward as she searched for the attacker.

He had disappeared.

Carth felt pressure on her shadow ability. It was the same sort of pressure she had recognized when she was in Asador, the pressure that told her someone with power was nearby, if not what their power was and how they could use it.

She pulled them to a nearby alley, remaining cloaked as she did. In the darkness of night, the cloaking wouldn't look quite as unusual. It wouldn't be quite as out of place.

The pressure surged against her again, and Carth rolled, a knife barely missing her once more.

She couldn't see the assassin, but he somehow managed to see her.

Either she needed to capture him, or she needed to follow him. Given the way he'd bested her the last time, she wasn't certain she could capture him. But could she follow him? Doing so might allow her to understand who had instructed him, who *really* had hired him.

She leaned into Marna, whispering in her ear, "I'm going to have to die."

Marna's eyes widened slightly.

Carth jumped away from the other woman, leaving her couched in shadows in the alley. Carth lowered her shadow cloaking, letting the connection to her magic disappear, and allowing the shadows to swirl around her. She resisted the urge to reach for the shadows, resisted the urge to reach for the power of the flame. Instead, she crept along the row of buildings.

At the end of the street, she noted Dara watching her. Carth smiled, a sad smile.

A knife whistled.

Carth twisted, slightly to the side.

The knife pierced her back, below her left shoulder blade, puncturing her lung.

As it sank in, Carth fell, flaring a hint of the flame, searing off the injury, trying to sear the poison off.

She dropped to the ground, unmoving.

Carth listened, uncertain whether she had made a mistake, if she would really die from this wound. It was possible that she would, in fact, die from it. It was possible that this had been a mistake.

She felt movement near her and, connected as she was to the flame, she could tell that it wasn't Dara, and it wasn't Marna. She could even tell that it wasn't Timothy.

No, this had the distinct sensation of her assassin.

When she didn't move, he hurried off, leaving her in the street, bleeding from a wound that would kill her.

CHAPTER 28

CARTH ROLLED OVER, THE KNIFE IN HER BACK throbbing. After the assassin had left, she'd used the power of the flame to heal herself, drawing upon it so that she could recuperate. It took significant strength for her to use that ability, and injured as she was, she very nearly overwhelmed her ability to recover. Not only did she fight the wound in her back, but she fought the poison the assassin had used, one that she'd only been able to fully counter because she'd kept a rolled leaf of narcass in her pocket. She'd stuffed it into her mouth when she'd observed the attacker.

If things went as she hoped, Marna would be following him, leaving a way for her to trail after.

Carth sat up, her head woozy from the effort. Had she made a mistake, allowing him to attack her this way? She didn't think so, but there was the real possibility that he might discover Marna.

A hand slipped underneath her arm, helping her stand.

Carth looked over to see Timothy holding on to her, a concerned expression across his face. "You shouldn't live."

Carth tried to laugh, but it hurt too much. "I shouldn't, but I am."

"Take this, then."

He handed her a vial of powder, and Carth eyed it suspiciously. "I promise that I will not poison you," Timothy said. "Besides, haven't I helped you often enough that I've proven myself to you?"

"It's a little difficult to trust someone."

"Yes. Sometimes it is difficult to trust. But sometimes we have no choice but to do so."

Carth unstoppered the powder and sniffed it.

"You only need a pinch."

"What does it do?"

"I suspect it does much the same as what your friend took."

"I'm concerned how it might interact with my—"

"You think you would be the first person with abilities to consume it? No, there have been plenty others who have used this combination. Plenty others who have enjoyed the augmentation this allows."

Carth tipped a little bit of the vial back, letting the powder settle into her palm. "Do I inhale it?"

Timothy shook his head with a smile. He reached into her palm, grabbed the powder, and stuck it into his cheek. "See? There's nothing to fear."

Carth took the powder, placing a pinch of it into her cheek as he had done, and felt an immediate jolt.

It was a burning sensation, one that reminded her of when she'd first attempted using the A'ras magic, only this came with a steady throbbing, one that she felt starting in her lips and working its way down her throat, before spreading out to her arms and her legs. It was not painful, despite the burning she noticed. This was… invigorating.

Power thrummed through her. It was the power of the A'ras magic, the power of the shadows, and they flowed together, combined by her, and given strength by whatever this concoction was.

Carth felt the power of the A'ras magic healing her, knitting together the damage the knife had caused to her back, burning off the poisoning.

"That was…"

Timothy nodded knowingly. "Yes. That was."

"Did you get to see him?"

Timothy nodded. "A dangerous game you are playing here, Carth. You could have died by that knife."

Carth frowned. "I knew I could counter the poisoning."

"It's not only the poisoning you need to fear. It's the man."

"Who is he?"

"Someone who trained with another like me. Someone who has significant knowledge and skill. He is not someone you should take lightly."

"Does he have abilities?"

"Not the same as you. His are of a different descent. Have you seen his green eyes?"

Carth nodded.

"They are a marker of his people." Carth remembered another man with green eyes, one who had attacked her, aligned with the Hjan. That couldn't be a coincidence, could it?

"Where are they from?" Carth asked.

"I thought you knew the Hjan," Timothy said. "You faced them before, you attacked them. And now you're asking about them?"

"Not the Hjan," Carth said. "Where are they originally from?"

"As I said, they're from a place along the coast, a place where the people have abilities of their own, nothing quite like your shadows or your ability with the flame. They have some with enhanced sight, some with the ability to hear things others could not, some with the ability to anticipate, almost as if they were seeing the future, and some with the ability to enter your mind and know your thoughts."

"And control them," Carth said. That had been the secret of the Hjan that she hadn't known. That had been what they had wanted to keep, but she'd seen how they used that ability to control others, attacking with it, forcing the Lashasn like Dara to act against her will. Forcing even those of Ih-lash to act against their will. They might not be able to acquire their abilities, but they could acquire those with those abilities. That was the secret the Hjan sought.

"And this man? You know who he is, don't you?"

Timothy nodded. "I know who he is. Most who work with the Caulad Guild know who he is. He has taken our teachings and twisted them. He has become a faithless man," Timothy said.

"Why do I think there's more to it than that?"

Timothy sighed. "Because I don't think we need your friend to know where he is going."

"Where's that?"

"To Thyr."

CHAPTER 29

CARTH AND TIMOTHY MOVED UNENCUMBERED THROUGH the streets of Thyr. They had traveled by ship, taking the *Goth Spald* along the coast, with Carth trusting that Timothy would do as he promised, and that he would help her find this man, that he would help her discover what secrets he sought in Thyr.

She hoped to find Marna, not wanting to come across this assassin before he came across her friend. But mostly wanting to find him before he reached the Hjan.

Timothy led her, knowing the streets, and Carth wondered briefly how he knew so well where he was going, but she also knew she needed to trust him. Timothy had been nothing if not honest with her. There was no reason to distrust him.

In that, Timothy was right, she did need to trust him.

Thyr was a massive city, one nearly the size of Asador, filled with sprawl and darkness, but also bright colors and lush greenery throughout the city, and a floral scent that hung over everything. People moved hurriedly, and she found the crowd somewhat unsettling, the way they were packed into the city more densely than even in Nyaesh.

"Why here?" Carth asked as they rounded a corner. The people within Thyr appeared no different than anyone else. Some seemed a little harder, some dirtier, but for the most part, it was a city in many ways like Asador. A massive tower of scholars existed outside of the city, and Timothy had shared with her that the Hjan were a part of that tower, that they had originally been those scholars. She didn't fully understand, but perhaps she didn't need to.

"Why here? Because this is where Venass had their start."

"Explain to me the difference between Venass and the Hjan?"

His eyes narrowed a moment. "You'll need to be careful using those terms in this place. People are understandably sensitive to both terms. But the Hjan are part of Venass, they support them, working as an arm of assassins, assigned to help enforce the rest of

Venass's agenda. And trust me when I tell you that they have an agenda."

"What agenda is that? Were they involved with the attacks in Asador? Were they trying to move women to sell them for slavery?" Carth didn't think that was the case; that seemed less than what Venass was interested in. They seemed more interested in acquiring power. Smuggling women, even though some of those women had power, when they had managed to hold her, seemed beneath the Hjan. But was it part of Venass's greater plan? Maybe that was the key that she didn't fully understand.

"There are only a few who truly know what Venass seeks. They are scholars, but what they study is a different sort of endeavor than what you would find in Asador."

"If that's the case, then they are after power. Knowing that, I can counter them."

"Think of the numbers you faced in Reva. Those were men enhanced with various combinations of leaves and roots and toxins, so that they could augment their natural abilities. Those of Venass—and those of the Hjan—they have a different power, oftentimes one that occurs naturally, that they augment with something."

"Something? Do you mean like your concoctions?"

"Not like the concoctions." He said the word with a slight distaste. Carth had noted how he preferred a more elegant term, much like he preferred the more elegant term *augment*. She smiled to herself, thinking that if anything, Timothy was someone she was beginning to understand.

"No, they use something different than what we use. We haven't yet learned the secret, but it is telling that most from Venass, and most of the Hjan, carry scars."

"Do they physically augment themselves?"

Timothy shrugged. "I can only speculate what they do. I'm not certain, and I'm not sure that anyone is certain enough to say what they do, and how they managed to augment themselves."

He fell silent as they turned the corner, and a massive temple rose up before them.

Carth had seen many temples within Nyaesh. Many were no longer used the way they once had been, people's faith changing, new gods taking the place of others, but this one had the look of age to it. There was activity in and out of the temple, some wearing flowing robes that she suspected indicated that they were priests of some sort. Others wore the garb of the people she'd seen within the city, and Carth presumed they were parishioners.

"Why here?" Carth asked.

"Because here is where our friend will have gone."

Timothy led them into the temple. The walls were made of a white marble. Sconces glowed with light.

Massive tapestries depicted scenes that seemed too fantastical to believe. A soft silence hung over everything, one where Carth felt compelled to keep a hushed voice. She managed to keep her footsteps muted as well. She began drawing upon the shadows, wanting to retreat into them, to cloak herself, when Timothy laid a hand on her arm and shook his head.

"Not here."

Carth wondered how he was aware of her ability, how he knew that she reached for them, but there were others who had been aware as well.

Timothy led them away from the main part of the temple, turning down a narrow hallway and pushing through a doorway. When the door shut behind them, Carth turned to him and, with a smile on her face, asked, "Are you some sort of priest?"

Timothy shrugged. "Perhaps by those here, I might be viewed as a priest, but not by any who know better."

"I'm not sure what that means."

"No. You do not."

They passed through another few doors, the halls turning before Carth began to lose track of where they were. The temple was enormous, with enough branching hallways that she wondered if Timothy intended to confuse her or if he was simply leading her someplace she had not yet discovered.

Finally, he stopped at a door and pushed it open. On the other side of the door, a man sat at a desk. He had a shorn head and a plain-looking face, and when he looked up, his eyes seemed penetrating. His gaze skipped from Carth to Timothy, settling on and holding on to the other man. There was no other expression on his face. He seemed almost disappointed to see Timothy here.

"You should not have come," the man said. He had a deep voice, one that would likely fill the halls of the temple. She could imagine him chanting the ceremony, his voice the voice of authority, the voice of whatever god these people believed in.

"He is here."

The man paused a moment before looking up. "Here? He should not be here. He knows better than to come here."

Carth noted Timothy's gaze flickering to her. What was taking place between these men? What was she missing?

"Are you certain?"

"Have you ever known me not to be certain?"

The bald man clasped his hands together on top of the desk and leaned forward. His face showed a flicker of emotion, a slight frown, but that disappeared within moments. "It would be unfortunate if he has come here."

"It was unfortunate that he chose to leave in the first place."

"Yes. Unfortunate. And why have you brought another into this?"

"Because he attempted to terminate her."

Carth waited, trying to take stock of what she observed here. There was something she wasn't quite grasping, and she was determined to understand what it was. It had to do with Timothy and whatever role he played. It seemed that Timothy was more complicated than she had known. There were other secrets he kept from her. She had believed him nothing more than a simple sellsword, but that seemed not to be the case. And perhaps there was nothing simple about Timothy.

"What would you ask of me?" the other man asked.

Timothy nodded, as if it had been a foregone conclusion that this other man would do what Timothy needed.

"I would have answers."

"What kind of answers?" the man asked.

Carth glanced to Timothy, noting the tight smile on his face. It made him appear even more dangerous, if that were possible. Carth had believed Timothy to be somewhat plain, inconspicuous, but when he made that face, he was anything but plain.

"We need to find him before he—"

The other man cut Timothy off with a shake of his head. "If it is as you say, then we truly do need to find him."

He turned to Carth, his eyes glittering. "You should take a moment to pray," he told her.

Carth shook her head. "I think you are mistaken. I don't—"

Timothy rested his hand on her arm, silencing her. "I will take her into the temple, and we will pray a moment."

The other man nodded once, and Carth frowned, thinking that she was still missing something.

CHAPTER 30

THE INSIDE OF THE TEMPLE WAS FILLED WITH A STEADY chanting, one that seemed to reverberate from the walls. It filled her, a pleasant, comforting chant, one that Carth found herself swaying with. Timothy sat with a rigid back in the booth next to her, saying nothing. They had been here for over an hour, neither of them saying anything, nothing but the soft, steady chanting around them.

Carth occasionally had an urge to reach for the shadows, but each time she started to do so, Timothy placed his hand on her arm, as if knowing what she did. Most likely he did, though Carth still wondered how. Was it related to the concoctions he used, or was there something else? Was there some other way he managed to detect her reaching for the shadows?

Perhaps Timothy had an ability of his own that she

had yet to determine. He had made it clear that many who used the concoctions had innate abilities, which was part of the reason he had known she would be safe when she had taken some of it.

It made her look at him with renewed interest. Here was a man she had met by chance, but one who not only had aided her in rescuing the women, stopping Guya and Hoga in the process, but now was somehow pivotal in whatever was taking place.

She felt movement down the aisle and looked over to see a young man dressed in a light blue robe coming towards her. He had each hand slipped into the sleeve of the opposite arm, and he stopped next to her, leaning forward.

Carth waited, wondering if he expected her to say something, or if he came to deliver some message to her.

When he didn't, Timothy reached past her and made a quick gesture with his fingers. The man nodded and pulled one hand from his sleeve, slipping a folded sheet of paper into Timothy's hands.

"May the light guide you, acolyte," Timothy said.

The acolyte nodded once and then turned before disappearing back down the aisle.

When he was gone, Timothy unfolded the paper, his eyes skimming the page. Creases formed in the corners of his eyes, and he stood. "We need to hurry."

Timothy swept down the aisle and out of the

temple. He said nothing more. Carth followed, uncertain what else to do, wondering what he might've seen on the page that would leave him worried like that.

Outside the temple, there was a steady sort of chaos in the streets. Carth raced to catch up with Timothy, reaching her shadows and the flame, no longer feeling compelled to restrict herself from accessing them. As she approached him, Timothy nodded, as if he agreed with her need to use both of her abilities.

He turned to her and handed a small vial to her. "You will want to take this."

"What did you learn?"

"This man that you follow, he has knowledge that we have sought to keep from Venass."

"Because he's one of the Caulad Guild?"

Timothy tipped his head. "Yes. If Venass is successful in recruiting him, we will lose much."

"What is this temple?" Carth asked. "It's more than simply the Caulad Guild."

Timothy glanced over. "It is more than that. I've told you that there are Hjan assassins. That is what this is. It's a network, one that has helped control the flow of power in this land for many years."

"And if he goes to the Hjan, it will disrupt the flow of power?"

"If he goes to the Hjan, it is possible that they will be the power."

"Then where are we going? What did you learn that

worries you?"

"Because he is going to the tower."

"The tower?" Carth couldn't conceal her confusion.

"Venass. The seat of their power. That is where he goes."

The tower rose up out of the ground, a giant finger of stone surrounded by an empty landscape. The city of Thyr stood behind them at a reasonable distance, as if the city itself intended to give the tower the necessary space. Timothy guided her, and neither of them spoke. Carth still hadn't seen any sign of Marna and had begun to wonder if the woman had become lost or if she had been harmed in the journey. She feared what might have happened to her as the assassin made his way to the tower.

Carth held on to the shadows, drawing them from her with a certain urgency. She feared much the same as Timothy, wanting to prevent the Hjan from gaining any more knowledge and power than they already had. If that meant that she had to stop this assassin, then she would.

As they raced towards the tower, she noted a single man making his way from Thyr along the road to the tower. He walked without any sense of urgency. He wore a dark cloak, and Carth could feel something coming from him. There was power, though she didn't understand the source.

The man turned, and even from this distance, she could see the glitter of his green eyes. When he saw her, he smiled.

"We should hurry," Carth said.

"I don't think it matters."

Carth realized that he was right. The man waited. He seemed unconcerned that Carth was here. He seemed unconcerned that he stood in the open countryside, outnumbered. He might even know that Timothy had some ability.

Carth and Timothy continued forward, and Carth held on to the shadows, drawing the flame as well, holding the powers within her as she approached.

"You don't die easily, do you?" he said.

"I can't let you reach the tower," Carth said.

"That will not be up to you."

"Who are you?" Carth asked.

The man shook his head. "Who I am no longer matters." His gaze flicked to Timothy. "Much like who I was no longer matters. It is who I will become that matters."

"Why?"

"They needed a demonstration. They pointed me to Asador."

They. The Hjan. Had Hoga somehow worked on their behalf?

"I won't let you reach the tower," Carth said.

"No?" the man asked, arching a brow. "You will stop me, but how will you stop them?" he asked.

A wave of nausea rolled through Carth's stomach.

She had felt it before, but it had been some time since she had detected the Hjan traveling near her. She called it flickering but knew they had another term for it, as Invar had called it traveling.

Where there had been an empty plain, now there were six men, each appearing in a flicker. They surrounded the assassin.

The assassin watched her with a lazy arrogance. "As I said, what will you do?"

Timothy reached for his sword, but this time, Carth rested a hand on his arm.

"You not going to fight them?" Timothy whispered.

Carth's gaze drifted past the assassin, drifted past most of the Hjan assembled around her, and fixed on one man, one with deep green eyes who she had seen before. Somehow, she knew that he led the Hjan.

"I suppose you will claim him?" Carth said.

The man tipped his head. "It's a move I believe you are familiar with, is it not?"

"You will abide by the accords. He will abide by the accords."

The green-eyed man only nodded. "I abide by them as long as you do."

"I claim the Caulad Guild," Carth said.

The green-eyed Hjan's gaze narrowed. "That was not the agreement."

Carth shrugged. "I claim them just the same. If you harm them, you will violate the accords."

The man nodded to the others around him. As one, they flickered, taking the assassin with him.

The green-eyed man stared at her, an amused expression on his eyes. "What game are you playing at?" he asked.

Carth shook her head. "This is no game. And I'm determined to protect the accords. All who follow me are under my watch. Any harm that comes to them, I will take it as an insult and a violation of the accords."

A hint of a smile played across his lips. "I have done nothing to violate the accords."

Carth frowned. "No. You have only seen that someone you sought to recruit did. If this tactic is employed again, I will consider it a violation."

The man tipped his head, and with a smile, he said, "Much like your violation?" He watched Carth, waiting for a reaction, but she refused to give him one. "I will see you again."

"I will look forward to it."

The man flickered, disappearing, leaving her and Timothy standing alone on the plane with the tower before them.

"What was that?" Timothy asked.

"That," Carth said, "is me ensuring our safety."

CHAPTER 31

THE STREETS OF ASADOR STILL FELT EMPTY, THE WAY they had felt in the days since Lindy's death. Carth still missed her friend, and still felt the pain of her loss on a daily basis, even now that she understood the reason it had happened. How Hoga had manipulated the situation, steering Marna toward a more dangerous choice. Marna had not known exactly what she was getting into when she had arranged for the assassin.

"Will you remain here?" Marna asked.

Carth glanced over to Marna. They stood crouched on a rooftop near the edge of the city, the docks visible. From here, Carth could see the movement of ships in and out of the harbor, and she had a sense of the smugglers working, as well as a sense of the women making up part of her network.

"I think I'll stay here for now," Carth said with a

sigh. "Eventually, I'm going to return to what I've started."

Continuing with what she had begun would be difficult. It would take time to continue to establish a network along the coast, but given what she'd learned, and what had happened outside of Thyr, she thought she had no choice but to continue. The Hjan made that abundantly clear.

"You're going to need help," Marna said.

"I am," Carth agreed.

"I can assist you in this."

They hadn't spoken about this part of Carth's plan during the remainder of their return to Asador. Marna had been silent, and thankfully unharmed.

"You don't need to do this. You have others you serve, and they need you just as much."

"The smugglers guild is fully established. I can continue my influence there, and can continue to help you as well. Unless…"

"Unless what?" Carth asked.

Marna shrugged. "Unless you would rather I not. I understand if you are still angry with me about what happened."

"I haven't decided how I feel about what you did. But I understand why you did what you did. It's a decision I might have made were I in your situation."

"And Hoga? What is your plan for her?"

Carth smiled to herself. "Hoga will be useful. She

might not agree with it now, but I think that in time, she will come around."

Carth had sequestered Hoga and intended to take everything that the woman knew from her. If nothing else, she would understand the Caulad Guild better. She would use everything she knew—everything she possessed—to ensure that Hoga no longer harmed anyone else. She would help, whether she liked it or not.

And there was the fact that Hoga had some connection to the Hjan. She had to have for them to have used her to find the assassin. She would learn what that connection was.

"Thank you," Marna said.

Carth frowned and looked over to her. "You're thanking me now?"

"I'm thanking you for saving my sister. You didn't have to do that. And I... I thought you were—"

"I know. We were used." Manipulated by Hoga. Perhaps Carth should play Tsatsun with her. Maybe it would help her understand the woman and the way she thought better.

Carth let out a long sigh. She was a long way from Nyaesh, and a long way from the person she had been when she had lived on the streets, scared and trying to understand what she'd seen, the horror that she had observed of her mother dying in front of her. When that had occurred, she had felt helpless, lost. That person was no more. Carth was powerful. With her connections to both the shadows and the flame, she had a responsibility to use those powers.

And there was much danger in the world. There were plenty of others who thought to abuse the powers they possessed. She had to do what she could for those without power.

Along the way, she intended to strengthen others. She needed the women she served to realize they were stronger than they knew. Already in Asador and in Reva, it was happening. Women had discovered that they had strength and power that they had never known. That discovery brought Carth much joy. It would be necessary for them to discover it, especially as they faced the growing threat of the Hjan.

"You should take some time to celebrate with those you helped," Marna said. "Sometimes it does us good to realize that we've impacted others."

"I think you need to come with me," Carth said.

Marna smiled. "That isn't my place."

"It will be if you intend to coordinate Asador for me."

Marna tipped her head to the side, studying Carth for a long moment. Her brow knitted, and after a while, she nodded. "That I can do. On one condition."

"You're going to place conditions on me now?"

Marna shrugged. "Only that you agree to continue to play Tsatsun with me."

Carth allowed herself to smile. "I think I would like that."

She gathered the shadows around her and jumped from the rooftop. Marna followed barely a step behind, enhanced by the concoctions that Hoga had taught her. Those were the concoctions that strengthened Carth and the women of Asador. They would grow stronger together. They would become more than what they had been.

For the first time since coming to Asador, Carth felt a glimmer of hope.

The Shadow Accords will continue. Sign up HERE to be the first to learn about new releases!

Looking for another great read? Soldier Son, Book 1 of The Teralin Sword, out now.

As the second son of the general of the Denraen, Endric wants only to fight, not the commission his father demands of him. When a strange attack in the south leads to the loss of someone close to him, only Endric seems concerned about what happened.

All signs point to an attack on the city, and betrayal by someone deep within the Denraen, but his father no longer trusts his judgment. This forces Endric to make another impulsive decision, one that leads him far from the city on a journey where he discovers how little he knew, and how much more he has to understand. If he can prove himself in time, and with the help of his new allies, he might be able to stop a greater disaster.

ABOUT THE AUTHOR

DK Holmberg currently lives in rural Minnesota where the winter cold and the summer mosquitoes keep him inside and writing.

Word-of-mouth is crucial for any author to succeed and how books are discovered. If you enjoyed the book, please consider leaving a review at Amazon, even if it's only a line or two; it would make all the difference and would be very much appreciated.

Subscribe to my newsletter to be the first to hear about giveaways and new releases.

For more information:
www.dkholmberg.com
dkh@dkholmberg.com

ALSO BY D.K. HOLMBERG

Servant of Fire

Born of Fire

Broken of Fire

Light of Fire

Cycle of Fire

Others in the Cloud Warrior Series

Prelude to Fire

Chasing the Wind

Drowned by Water

Deceived by Water

Salvaged by Water

The Endless War

Journey of Fire and Night

Darkness Rising

Endless Night

Summoner's Bond

Seal of Light

The Lost Garden

Manufactured by Amazon.ca
Bolton, ON

20018046R00166